D0942961

The Delicate Pioneer

THE DELICATE PIONEER

A Novel

Sally Watson

iUniverse, Inc.

New York Lincoln Shanghai

The Delicate Pioneer

Copyright © 2007 by Sally Watson

All rights reserved. No part of this book may be used or reproduced by any means, graphic, electronic, or mechanical, including photocopying, recording, taping or by any information storage retrieval system without the written permission of the publisher except in the case of brief quotations embodied in critical articles and reviews.

iUniverse books may be ordered through booksellers or by contacting:

iUniverse
2021 Pine Lake Road, Suite 100
Lincoln, NE 68512
www.iuniverse.com
1-800-Authors (1-800-288-4677)

This is a work of fiction. All of the characters, names, incidents, organizations, and dialogue in this novel are either the products of the author's imagination or are used fictitiously.

ISBN-13: 978-0-595-42506-8 (pbk)
ISBN-13: 978-0-595-86840-7 (ebk)
ISBN-10: 0-595-42506-2 (pbk)
ISBN-10: 0-595-86840-1 (ebk)

Printed in the United States of America

Dedicated to fellow-ailurophile
and friend of many lives,
Harriet Ann Kaplan

CONTENTS

▼

CHAPTER 1

▼

THE DREADFUL SECRET

"There now, li'l missy!" Viola's dark loving hands tucked Felicity into her high bed, smoothing the counterpane and then the long mouse-brown ringlets lying limply over the ruffled night dress. "You jes' lie there and rest. Too much excitement and too much dinner." Viola stooped massively to pick up the lacy froth of petticoats, pantalettes and pink ruffled frock from the polished floor. "I done tol' your mama it would be too much for you. Jes' too much Christmas, that's all."

Leaving the tall candles burning, she slipped out, and Felicity leaned against the high goose-down pillows, feeling as limp as her too-fine hair, and cross about both. It wasn't fair! God could have made her healthy, or her hair thick or curly or golden: she'd have settled for any one of them. Adelaide's hair was all three, and she enjoyed glorious health, besides, while Felicity had always been sickly. She didn't think she liked God very well, though she had never mentioned this to anyone, least of all God.

But while Viola had been quite right about the drawing room being so hot (and Felicity could never take heat) that was only part of the reason she'd suddenly been taken poorly on this Christmas night of 1851. The other part was— *it*. Felicity didn't know what *it* was, but for nearly a month now it had made Papa silent and frowning, and Mama tearful and afraid. And when Aunt Julia and Uncle Jonathan came over today for Christmas, Felicity had at once seen that they knew, too. Even Cousin Charles and Adelaide knew. Only Felicity didn't. It wasn't fair!

It wasn't so bad Charles knowing: he was fifteen. But Adelaide was twelve, only a few months older than Felicity. It was always like this. Adelaide got everything! She was beautiful and healthy and clever and talented and angelically good, and was told secrets, while Felicity had none of these things. Even Mama, who fussed over Felicity as if she were the only little girl in the world, often pointed out Adelaide's virtues—as if Felicity couldn't see for herself that her detestably perfect cousin could ride, embroider, play the spinet and dance, and that the boys always clustered adoringly around her, and that the whole world loved and admired her. Except Felicity, who deplorably failed to appreciate her good fortune in having such a cousin.

There was a light step in the room. Felicity turned her head and regarded that cousin bleakly.

"I just came up to see how you feel, honey," said Adelaide with great sympathy. "I'll sit here on your bed and cheer you up for a while; I don't mind a bit." Perching on the side of the feather-quilted four-poster, she patted Felicity's thin hand tenderly with her own dimpled one. Her golden curls fell thickly over green silken shoulders as she leaned forward—reminding Felicity that she herself was too sallow to wear green, that and her own ringlets were of the rag-curls-always-coming-out variety. (Viola said her hair might curl a bit if it were cut short, but Mama had had conniptions at the idea. Short hair was not ladylike.)

"—don't you think?" finished Adelaide.

Felicity blinked. "What?"

Adelaide, accustomed to an attentive audience, frowned a little. "I said," she repeated with sweet patience, "that you really aren't strong enough for either journey, but your mama's probably right that the overland trip would be better, for you'd surely get dreadfully seasick."

Felicity's brown eyes darkened and widened in her thin face, and her heart began pounding heavily. "What trip?" she whispered.

Now it was Adelaide's lovely blue eyes that opened wide. "Goodness! Don't you know, F'licity? I thought you did. I reckon I shouldn't have said anything."

This was *it*! Felicity know it was! "Tell me!" she commanded, her small, sharply-cut lips beginning to quiver in a way that meant she could easily become hysterical if thwarted. Adelaide gave in, not too reluctantly.

"Well, honey," she began, "it's all just perfectly dreadful. Both of our fathers made a big investment in a gold mine in California, and it was a cheat, and all of our money is gone, or at least most of it. We have to sell our plantations and all the slaves, and we can't just stay around here and be paupers, so we're all going Out West."

Felicity's world wheeled dizzily around her and then settled down a bit, and she found to her surprise that she wasn't as upset as she ought to be. For one thing, she had been imagining far worse things, and for another, it was a relief just knowing what it was, and for a third—

"Father says we should go to Oregon Territory," Adelaide went on. "He says that's the modern Promised Land, and California's too rough now with the gold rush going on. But your mama is terribly upset, especially about your health, and Charles doesn't want to leave his school yet. First they thought just the menfolk would go by covered wagon, and get settled and then send for us females to come by ship. But Father doesn't want us to travel without a man, so Charles should stay and finish the year, and come with us. But then your mama said she won't be separated from your papa; and anyway, sailing all that way around South America would be the death of you; and besides she's sure the ship would sink; so now Mother and Charles and I will stay with Aunt Gertrude, and Father and your family are going by wagon and when you-all find a good place and have a nice house, he'll send for Mother and Charles and me, and we'll come by ship. It will be much nicer than a dirty old covered wagon, but I reckon you'll just have to be brave about it, honey. It's all settled."

She regarded Felicity with lively sympathy. But Felicity looked unaccountably philosophical about it. In fact, she looked downright pleased. Adelaide was puzzled, since it never occurred to her that Felicity would have preferred tunneling underground to traveling with her cousin.

Of course, once she had a day or two to think about it, Felicity was horrified. She was going to lose everything she knew, even Viola and her lovely frilled bedroom, and the other slaves; and the trip sounded altogether terrifying.

Mama made it more so by wailing and crying. Papa tried to help.

"Cheer up, honey-child, maybe it won't be so hot out West; you know you hate the heat. And think how interesting it will be."

Far too interesting, it turned out.

The trip had been like something a vengeful God would invent for a choice corner of hell. First, leaving Viola; then the tangled forests and mud and dangerous river crossings to Independence, Missouri—which was only the start, it turned out. It would take another six months to walk the further two thousand miles to the Pacific. And they did all walk it (except for the drivers of the wagons, and babes and frail Felicity) through more dangerous river crossings; dust, heat, hunger, thirst, dysentry, Indians (who had, in fact, turned out to be least of their worries) exhaustion, broken axles, dead oxen, most of their furniture and belongings left behind one by one to join the clutter of abandoned goods along the trail, and finally cholera. The relatively easy crossing of the Rockies by the South Pass was only a reprieve, followed by deadly desert, a foot deep in dust, lined with gravestones.

And now Felicity slumped on the tailboard of her uncle's covered wagon, leaning her dusty head against the side, looking around with dulled eyes at the activity surrounding her. Within the circle of wagons, all the other people in the train were busily making camp. They were lean, shabby, and covered with dust— but sparkling with exuberance. They'd got through the desert at last! Over the worst of it now, they told one another cheerfully. Almost there! Now there was practically nothing between them and Oregon City: only a few hundred more miles of mountains, forests, rivers and general wilderness. But no more deserts: Mr. Mercer had said so.

Felicity loooked at them incredulously. Through the layers of dust, her mousy plaits and pasty face looked even more mousy and pasty than usual, matching the gloom of her spirits. How could they all be so heartless? Mama and Papa were dead of the cholera, buried back yonder beyond the Rockies. Felicity had survived, to everyone's astonishment, but sometimes she almost wished she hadn't. She was still weak from cholera and grief, and she ached all over from the endless jouncing of the springless wagon. Probably she had a fever; certainly she felt very poorly indeed, and also extremely sorry for herself.

Well, no one else did, now Mama and Papa were dead. She was just a nuisance and a burden, no one loved her except maybe Uncle Jonathan just a little, and she really wished she had never been born. She sighed, uncomforted by the cool green of this lovely valley, or Mr. Mercer's shout that they would rest here for a day or two.

Rejoicing, men now unhitched the teams and led them off to water and grass. Women began unpacking food and kettles, eyeing the grimy clothing and the stream with a purposeful air. The other children were all busy, too, racing around gathering firewood, chattering with an energy and cheer that caused Felicity to look at them with resentment.

"My pa is the best leader of any wagon train that ever was!" shouted young Susan Mercer (whose ninth birthday was either just coming or just gone, depending on whether September 30 had happened yet) from behind an armload of wood that rendered her round face almost invisible. "I'll bet," she added, letting it crash to the ground, "that he's the very first one ever to get his whole party across that horrible old desert without even one person dying." She glinted hazel eyes at Becky Horton, who at once rose to the challenge.

"What about Arne Knudsen's pa, and Mrs Gould, and Mr. and Mrs. Dare?"

The mention of her folks caused Felicity's tears to flow, as Eliza Mercer jumped to her sister's defense. "That was cholera!" she cried, honey braids tossing indignantly. "Pa told everyone not to drink water straight from the river; he couldn't help it if some sill—" She glanced fleetingly at the Dare wagon, softened her remark. "—some folks did it anyway. And most people didn't, so we had hardly any cholera compared to most parties. Remember how men were always riding back along the trail saying they had dozens and dozens sick with it?"

"Anyhow," put in Susan, "that was before we even reached the Rockies, and I said desert, and we didn't lose anyone there, did we? And I reckon most trains did."

That had, in fact, been painfully evident from the number of graves along the trail. Clarence Bagley and Becky claimed ghoulishly to have counted a hundred and twenty in one day. Now, Susan having won the argument, they all dropped their wood in the center of the wagon circle, drew grateful breaths of the sweet cool air, and reassured one another again that the worst was over.

"Pa says so." Eliza was a bit younger than Felicity, but a very aggressive young lady, just the most suitable type for pioneering. "He studied lots and lots about Oregon Territory, you know; that's how he knew he wanted to go to Puget Sound. He even had a dream about standing on a big woody hill with salt water on one side and fresh water on the other, and—"

"We know!" chorused the other young'uns, who had heard the story for the last five months, ever since they'd left Independence; and off they raced for more wood, leaving Felicity brooding after them. All right for *them*. *They* hadn't lost their folks. *They* didn't have delicate health. They'd been able to run and play and explore alongside the trail all they wanted, while Felicity had to sit in the jolting wagon day after day and week after week, bored and aching and almost wishing Mama didn't take quite such good care of her.

She leaned harder, closed her eyes, remembering. Was this September? Anyway, they'd departed from Virginia at the end of a mild February, and it was nearly May when the Bethel train had crossed the Missouri River and left the United States behind, and entered hell.

She dragged herself away from the disagreeable past to the disagreeable present, shifted her aching bones on the hard seat of the wagon tail, thrust out her lower lip and set about disliking God. Her head felt hot. She was probably coming down with cholera all over again, and if she died nobody would care, even herself.

"Well, well, Felicity Ann." It was Reverend Bagley, whose kindness was of the stiff-backbone variety. "Are you thanking God for our safe deliverance from the fiery desert?" He smiled, but Felicity, who definitely wasn't thanking God for anything, regarded him dourly. "I know," he said more gently. "You're grieving for your parents. But remember that they are much happier in heaven, my dear. And you should be grateful that God spared you, and that you still have your dear uncle to raise you as a father."

He patted her head kindly and went on. Felicity glowered after him unevenly, one brow flattened and the other bending toward her short nose. He didn't make sense. If it was all that lovely in heaven, why should she be grateful she wasn't there? Especially since not being there meant being here, feeling poorly all the time, and looking forward to being with Adelaide for all her born days; and the very best she could hope was that it would take simply years for her aunt and cousins to get here.

A tow-haired boy of fourteen appeared suddenly, looked at Felicity, raised an eyebrow.

"Feeling poorly as usual, Missy-Flissy? Why not see if you can stagger down to the stream and wash your dirty face? It might make you feel better."

She transferred the glower, remembering another grievance she had against God. Arne Knudsen! From the very first time he saw her, at Independence, he had been picking on her, calling her Dollbaby and Missy-Flissy, making it quite clear that he had no use for girls in general and less than none for helpless sickly ones. It had been bad enough just being in the same wagon train with him. Now it was worse. When Arne's pa died, Uncle Jon asked him to live with them until Arne was old enough to stake a claim for himself. Even after Aunt Julia and the others came. So that Felicity was going to have Arne and Adelaide instead of Mama and Papa!

She sobbed.

Arne, who was no more enthusiastic about Felicity than she was about him, hastily departed. He was sick of her delicate health, and he couldn't stand people who felt sorry for themselves, and he reckoned that what she needed was less pampering and more teasing. He applied the teasing every chance he got, but so far it hadn't seemed to make much difference. Possibly she really was just sickly and fretful by nature, and couldn't help it. He ran a hand through the dustiness of his thick hair and grinned crookedly. The whole Dare family, he reflected, seemed about the last people in the world who ought to be pioneers. They lacked stamina. Even Mr. Dare—now Uncle Jon—was neither sturdy nor practical. He could overlook the most obvious things! And though he innocently believed Arne needed him, actually, it was the other way around. It suited Arne to let him think so: he was very fond of Uncle Jon.

Down by the stream Mr. Mercer was leading his team back toward the wagons and having trouble with the restive white stallion Charlie. Arne ran down the slope to lend a hand, and then took the docile Tib while Mr. Mercer grinned his thanks.

"Arne-on-the-spot," he remarked. I hope you and Jonathan have decided to come all the way to Puget Sound with us. You're going to be a good man to have around."

Arne's ears reddened with pleasure. "Oh, you've sold us on it," he said. "Only I think you've overdone it, sir. I think Uncle Jon expects some kind of paradise. I mean—Well, he does know it's wilderness, but I think he pictures a sort of Eden; you know, all flowers and no snakes."

Tom Mercer chuckled. "I'm afraid a lot of them do. I wouldn't worry about Jonathan, though. He's a good man. Not very muscular, or even practical, but he's got intelligence and a kind of inner strength I like."

Arne nodded. They tethered the horses and went back to the wagon circle where Mrs. Mercer had apparently got Felicity down to the the steam for a cool wash, and was now settling her down with a bit of mending, for the girls and women were kept busy these days patching the patches.

Jonathan set down two buckets of water, stopped for an affectionate word with his niece, and ambled over to join Arne and Mr. Mercer.

"Nearly there now?" he suggested, his long face tired but hopeful, "Well—not quite," admitted Mr. Mercer, jerking his head toward the range of sharp-peaked mountains that barred their way to the west. "Still, once we get on the other side of those, it should be a fairly easy stretch to Portland, partly by river. Puget Sound is about a hundred and fifty miles further north, I gather."

Jonathan gave his good-natured chuckle. "Doesn't sound like much after we'll have come three thousand," he pointed out. "I wonder when I should send for my wife and children?"

Arne lifted his eyebrow. "Better wait until you've staked a claim," he suggested kindly. "Otherwise, how could you tell them where to find you?"

"That's right, agreed Jonathan in faint surprise. "A good thing I've your practical mind around, Arne—even if it was a sad loss that brought us together. But never mind. The worst is over now." And he went off to make sure Felicity wasn't getting chilled.

But the gods of fate had one last ironic slap for the Bethel wagon train. After surviving the whole hard trip with sweet smile and helping hand, after escaping cholera and aches and scorpions and hunger and thirst, after getting across the final terrifying Cascade mountain range, Mrs. Mercer caught pneumonia at Upper Cascade and died—leaving her husband and four motherless little girls stunned with grief.

Chapter 2

▼

The Patchwork Pup

Oregon Territory, Felicity grumbled to herself, was a good deal damper than a Promised Land ought to be. True, it was a welcome relief from the awful dry burning heat of prairie and desert, but she was in no mood to be pleased by anything.

And it was easy enough to be displeased by Portland, a city of some two thousand souls living in rough cabins and not at all engaged in anything like gracious living. Mama would have had conniptions. She would have hated the damp, too. A chilly damp. Felicity was glad for the warmth of the new woollen frocks, tight-waisted and full-skirted, that Mrs. Bagley had made for her. Mrs. Bagley had told Uncle Jon firmly that whatever little girls might wear in Virginia, pink frills and lace were not the thing for Oregon Territory. Felicity, who had never cared for either pink or ruffles, was pleased with the clear dark red and the soft blue of her new frocks.

She was wearing the red one now, with plain stoutly-made pantalettes and several layers of wool stocking, petticoat, mantles and shawls covering everything but her face, and making it difficult to move even had she felt like it. But Uncle Jon had told her to stay here and watch the luggage, so here she sat on top of her battered trunk on the open deck of the little ship, staring out across the astonishing dark green of this wild new world.

Near the rail Uncle Jon and Mr. Mercer talked earnestly. On the other side of the narrow deck the four Mercer girls wandered about, gazing around with interest but still subdued by the death of their mother. Mary Jane held small Alice firmly by the hand and kept an eye on Eliza and Susan, who were standing on tiptoe to peer over the rail at the Willamette River rushing by. Felicity wished she were better friends with them. She hadn't had much chance before, cooped in the wagon while they played with Becky Horton and Clarence and Susannah Bagley. Now she felt they had something in common. She wished they would come over and talk to her now. It never occurred to her to go over and talk to them.

She sighed. Gulls wheeled and yelped overhead, looking and sounding vaguely different from the ones back east. Mount Hood to the east brooded behind lowering clouds. The air was very damp indeed. But at least it had stopped raining— for the moment.

She glanced without interest at the Weekly Oregonian, which Uncle Jon had bought before boarding. It said that this was October 23, 1852; that a Chinook dictionary (whatever that was) had now been published in Portland; and that the stumps in the streets were being newly white-washed to prevent collisions in the dark. Felicity sniffed and turned her attention to a large seagull who perched on the rail staring at her with great interest. It was the closest she had ever been to a wild bird, and she stared back at the bold curious eyes with wonder. What was it thinking?

Presently it spread wide wings, rose into the air with enviable ease, and left nothing more interesting to watch than square-bearded Mr. Mercer, still talking to Uncle Jon.

"No," he was saying, "this is really the only solution. Seems we can't take the wagons the rest of the way: there's no roads yet. So it's foot or ship, and Felicity could never make it by foot: they say it's still a rough trail. So you're lucky to find this brig going up the coast. And," he added cheerfully, "I'm lucky to have met Dr. Maynard—"

"I wish we were going on this boat with you," said a wistful voice by Felicity's ear. It was Susan, her round eyes still filled with sadness. "I don't see why we can't if you can."

"Because Felicity has Mr. Dare and Arne both to take care of just one of her," said Mary Jane firmly, although her mouth drooped. "There are four of us, and someone would have to take us in until Pa finds his claim and files it and builds a house. And that's too much. Don't fuss, Susan; it just makes it harder for Pa. Better for us to spend the winter in Salem with his friends, and the Hortons will be there too, and then Pa will come for us in the spring, and—" Her voice faltered.

Felicity looked at her with complete sympathy. It was awful to lose your mother, said the two pairs of young and stricken eyes. Even worse when everything was unsettled and you hadn't even a home. "I wish you were coming with us," she said impulsively. "I wish—" She stopped, not knowing how to say that she wanted to be friends.

But Mary Jane looked as if she understood. "Never mind, we'll be coming later, and then you can show us around and everything."

Felicity nodded, quite liking the idea. "But if it's such an awful trip by land, why isn't your Pa coming up on the ship with us?"

"Well, because he has to take us to Salem, and find board for the horses, silly!" said the forthright Eliza. Felicity flushed.

"Hush up, Eliza," said Mary Jane. "Ma wouldn't have liked you to be rude. Anyhow, that isn't the only reason. Pa wants to try the overland trail and see how bad it really is for horses; and there's this Doc Maynard; he lives up there, and he's only just come down for a convention that's deciding things like counties and towns. He wants to tell them to let north of the Columbia River be a separate territory from Oregon, and that sort of thing. And when he goes back, he'll take Father and show him the way so they can fetch Tib and Charlie and the wagon next spring. He's awfully keen on that, because they don't have a team and wagon up there, and they really need it for the new lumber industry they want to start, with a sawmill and everything. And it looks like that town is where we'll all set-tle."

Felicity nodded, but her dark brows puckered in the lopsided frown that she didn't suspect she had. "I thought Dr. Maynard was coming with us. Uncle Jon said we were to stay with him when we got there."

"No," said Susan importantly. "It's a Mr. Denny who's going with you."

Eliza offered her bit of information. "But you might stay in Dr. Maynard's house for a bit; I heard him tell Father that."

Felicity promptly pictured a large white-columned colonial mansion, com-plete with verandas and wide velvet lawns and beautiful spare bedrooms. She had no trouble at all fitting it into a clearing in the wilderness, with other smaller estates around. There would be an army of slaves who would fuss over her and give her a hot bath and warm milk and tuck her into a four-poster bed with crisp linen sheets, and—

Her pleasant dream was interrupted by what seemed at first to be an army gone berserk. Shouts, stamping boots, yelps and waving arms swarmed up the gangplank in pursuit of a large animated something-or-other that tore excitedly around the deck and vanished behind Felicity's trunk. She pulled up her feet just in case, peered over long enough to decide that it was some sort of hairy animal, and turned back to face a young man with sandy hair, an older one with octagonal steel-rimmed glasses resting comfortably on his forehead, and an excited Arne.

"Where'd he go?" Arne demanded.

Felicity's eyes glinted. "Who?" she asked innocently.

"Dog," said the young man. "I think he's behind there."

"Couldn't be," said Arne positively. "Flissy'd be having conniptions if it were." He turned to search behind the cabin. The eyes under the glasses twinkled mischievously at Felicity, and their owner doffed his hat. "Would you be Miss Dare? I'm Doc Maynard, and very pleased to meet you. This is Arthur Denny, who'll be sailing with you. And that disreputable bundle of fur behind your trunk is the dog I've just been given in lieu of a doctor's fee for a birthing." He rolled his eyes heavenward. "Happens quite often. But this time I felt young Arne might be a better owner for it." Arne reappeared looking distracted, the Mercer girls behind him "I fancy he's right here, Arne. Come on out, boy! Here, you great lug."

The great lug barked and peered out doubtfully, clearly not at all sure whom to address as his Pack-leader. That one? he wondered, and lalloped diffidently toward Jonathan, who looked considerably startled.

Well he might. It was the most peculiar looking dog ever seen, apparently mixing a dozen breeds in one. His coat was like a drunken patchwork quilt. There was a white spot above one eye, a black patch covering the other, a mottled muzzle. The brown ear stood jauntily upright like a German Shepherd's; the charcoal one flopped over as if unduly influenced by a spaniel. The rest of him was an assortment of all these colours. Most of him had wire-terrier hair—except for his silken underbelly and a long plumed tail which waved frenziedly. His eyes were brown and soulful. He bounced in front of Jonathan, hopeful but uncertain.

"What is it?" asked Jonathan feebly.

"My new dog!" Arne strode over and took hold so commandingly that the pup at once recognized his Pack-Leader and began slobbering over His hands with a tongue like a yard of wet pink flannel.

"Mercy!" said Jonathan. The tongue reached successfully for Arne's face, and he backed off, wiping it. Felicity giggled. Mr. Mercer squatted for a closer look, defending his own face.

"Your doing?" he asked Doc Maynard severely. "Well, congratulations, Arne, and what will you do with it when it grow up?"

"Grows up?" Several pairs of eyes stared at the dog, already large, who bounced again at all the attention.

"Grows up! Look at his feet, you idiots; they're nearly as big as Felicity's!"

They looked. It was true. "He's going to grow up to them, isn't he?" said Jonathan resignedly. "Oh, well, at least he should scare off anything wild that dares come near. What's his name, this puppy of yours?"

Doc shrugged and looked at Arne, who screwed up his face. Suddenly names were flying around the deck. King. Goliath. Spot. Prince. Hero. Sampson. Traveller. Hash. Monster. Rags. Patches. Bones. Medley. None of them seemed quite right.

"Avast, there!" boomed a new voice, and a large barrel thumped itself to the deck a few feet from Felicity, who jumped. The puppy leaped up and barked excitedly, thinking it a new game. Arne grabbed his scruff. The men turned to Felicity, concerned.

"Are you all right, honey?" asked Uncle Jon. "You're not cold? Reckon you should go down to the cabin?"

Felicity shook her head firmly. For one thing, it was far too interesting here, and for another, the cabin smelled of fish and a stinky stove and too many people. She had the feeling she was going to stay on deck as much as possible, even if she froze to death. Eliza, who had briefly stuck her head into the cabin, giggled. "Don't blame you," she whispered.

Another barrel came down alongside the first. Some of the sailors climbed up the two swaying masts and did things with ropes, but they didn't let out the sails, to Susan's disappointment. More cargo and people were boarding, and the burly captain kept booming orders and occasionally using language that Mama wouldn't at all have approved. The five girls watched in silence, Arne conversed with his puppy, and Mr. Mercer with Uncle Jon. Presently Doc stopped staring out at the hills and river and mist.

"I think we'd best go ashore," he told the Mercers. "You folks had better get settled in the cabin, too, before all the berths are taken. We'll see you at New York Alki just as soon as we can get there. Good luck."

"Good-by," said Mary Jane wistfully, and "Good-by," echoed Felicity even more forlornly. It was just part of her ill luck that as soon as she began to be friends with someone, they were separated.

She stood sorrowfully by the rail while Arne got some rope for his puppy and then helped Uncle Jon take some of their things down to the cabin and lay claim to three of the berths that ran two-high around the sides. There were not many passengers, but they would all have to cook and eat and sleep right in that space; and Felicity fervently hoped that they'd be nice, the trip short, and by some miracle the weather nice enough so she could stay on deck most of the time. But remembering all the awful things Mama had said about travelling by ship, she prepared herself for the worst.

Chapter 3

▼

New York Alki

There was an explosion of activity aboard the ship. With creaks and rattles the sails were hoisted and the anchor broken out. With a shudder and a shake the Exact cast off and began dropping northward down the Willamette toward the Columbia River. The other half-dozen passengers, all going to Olympia, were down in the cabin. Felicity stood between Uncle Jon and Arne at the port rail, torn between interest and apprehension. So, apparently, was the puppy, if loud whining and vigorous tail-rotating were anything to go by.

The wind was very strong and—of course—damp. Might she get Galloping Consumption, as Mama always feared she would? A wisp of fine hair loosed itself and blew across her cheek. She brushed it back and looked with annoyance at Arne, who was sniffing the wind rapturously, his thick hair standing up in a blond crest.

"Holy Moses!" he said to Uncle Jon. "This is grand!" Arne had never been on a ship before; never even seen the sea. But now the blood of Viking ancestors rose in him, causing his blue eyes to glow with a brand new love. Well, two loves, counting the nameless pup. Even the minor annoyance of Missy-Flissy couldn't bother him now. He grinned down at her and tugged a skimpy braid in what was intended to be a kindly gesture.

Felicity, deep in the first symptoms of Galloping Consumption, didn't notice anything in the least kindly about having her hair pulled for no reason at all. It was just the way Arne always picked on her, and she'd have to put up with it for years and years—if she lived, that was ... Tears overflowed.

Arne gave a disgusted snort. "We never have drought for long with Dollbaby around, do we?" he jeered, and turned his attention back to his wriggling over-sized puppy, who instantly licked his face. Jonathan glanced over. He sometimes thought Arne and Felicity perhaps weren't quite as good friends as they might be. Sighing, he turned his attention to Arthur Denny, who was just coming along the deck towards him.

From somewhere behind came the voice of the burly, red-faced captain. "Hullo, there, Denny!" he boomed. "How's that big city of yours?" And he guffawed at some joke of his own. "Are these the sturdy new citizens, eh?" And he clapped Jon and Arne hugely on the shoulders.

"Oof!" said Jonathan, staggering slightly. The puppy, perceiving that his Pack Leader was being attacked, bared baby teeth in the very best snarl he knew, calculated to make the enemy retreat at once.

Alas, the captain never knew he had been intimidated. Roaring with amusement, he sauntered down the deck, and the objects of his merriment looked at one another ruefully. "It's true, I'm afraid; two thirds of the strapping newcomers aren't very strapping," murmured Jonathan a bit apologetically.

If Arthur Denny was dismayed by his diffidence and Feliciy's wan face, he hid it very well. "Are you really going to settle in New York Alki?" he asked hopefully. Felicity, confused, wiped out her vision of a plantation, and substituted the print of New York from one of Papa's books, as Mr. Denny continued. "We'll be delighted to have a few more citizens. "And we'll all pitch in to put you up until you get your own place built." He grinned wryly after the retreating captain. "Captain Johnson has a misplaced sence of humour," he observed. "The Big City is his idea of a joke. Never mind, we'll have the last laugh, for it will be a big city some day. It must be the finest port north of San Francisco, and not right on the coast, you know; accessible by ocean, but protected twice over from ocean storms. There's the Sound; and then a big bay with deep shipping water right up to the shore. And a river to the south—" His blue eyes sparkled. Clearly he was off on a pet theme. "Shipbuilding! Lumber to San Francisco! Furs and salmon to the United States!"

The print of New York wavered. Should it be lawns and magnolia trees around the plantation, after all?

"What's Alki?" asked Arne curiously, shifting his restless pet to his other arm and wondering what he'd weigh when he was grown. "You said New York Alki."

"Alki's a Chinook word: means by-and-by. Chinook's the trade jargon we use a lot up there; a combination of English, French and Indian. We haven't really settled on a proper name yet. Some of us want to name it after the Indian chief who's been such a good friend to us. Just wait 'til you meet him, Dare—"

Felicity sighed, cut the colonial mansion in half, and doubtfully substituted Indians for slaves. It didn't look right. The magnolias looked self-conscious, somehow. Perhaps—She lifted her gaze to the hills and mountains ranging to the north, east and south, bristling with giant fir trees so thick that you couldn't see a speck of ground between. They were proud, austere, almost black under the gray sky. And then a hesitant flicker of sunlight sped from hilltop to hilltop and touched them with magical gold-green. Mystery and enchantment! Something in Felicity woke and thrilled to it. She took out the magnolias and put in firs.

"—a mild climate," Mr. Denny finished, and turned to Arne, his narrow face split suddenly with a sympathetic grin. "Like the ship, do you? Me, too; I always sail when I can. Watch this, now; we're coming into the Columbia."

The ship surged forward as the Willamette poured into the incredible width of the Columbia River. Deep jade and pewter-gray and silver-blue, at least ten times wider than the Mississippi at Independence, it stretched endlessly ahead, plunging forward with a power that caused Arne to grip the rail with delight. The ship freshened and bucked in the current, and Felicity's eyes rounded apprehensively. She clutched Uncle Jon's arm with a small squeak.

"What's the matter, honey?" he asked in concern. "You fixing to be seasick?"

Felicity concentrated. She stared at the river. Her stomach lurched. She thought of the cabin and it lurched harder. "No," she said grimly through gritted teeth.

Arne turned a mocking eye. "Oh, come now, Missy-Flissy," he jibed. "You're just not trying."

Offended, she turned to her uncle for defense, but he just smiled vaguely and seemed to be thinking of something else. Where was his Southern chivalry? Scowling, she considered several scathing remarks, opened her mouth—and stopped. Blinked for a moment at the puppy, who, now limp in Arne's arms, was looking rather like Felicity had threatened to feel. If—She looked again, cheered up, smiled seraphically, turned a scornful shoulder to stare out at some charming gulls pacing the ship—and waited.

Arne stared in puzzlement. A moment later he received the pup's entire breakfast down the front of his chest.

"He's trying for both of us, I reckon," said Felicity sweetly. "And I really think you should name the poor thing, Arne. How about Barf?"

Arne glared at her, outraged, the biter bit. "No! He's—uh—King."

But it was too late. The name was was entirely too apt, and Barf remained Barf to the end of his days.

On and on they sailed, down the still-widening, island-dotted Columbia, first north and then west, until it stretched some ten miles from bank to bank. And then they were out in a shifting world of gray-green and taupe that was the Pacific Ocean. The motion instantly changed. The crew raced around, climbing masts and doing interesting things at top speed, while the ship heaved and pitched and galloped and fell into troughs between waves in a fashion that caused Felicity a certain amount of alarm until she got used to it. But though her stomach was uneasy a good deal of the time, she never did get really seasick. For one thing, she discovered that when she enjoyed the swooping so that her muscles and mind somehow encouraged the motion, her stomach seemed to accept it. And Mr. Denny peered gravely into her eyes one day and informed her that she belonged to the rare physical type Philo-Neptunius, to whom seasickness was quite impossible.

It was a pity that Barf didn't. He was appallingly seasick for the entire journey, usually down the front of Arne, who found that though he had a good stomach for sailing, it was less dependable for things like sick pups. Between one thing and another, Arne enjoyed the trip rather less than Felicity, which wasn't fair. He was the one with Viking blood, and now he hadn't even the time to properly savor either the trip or the probably-brief respite from Felicity's moaning. He cuddled Barf—no, King!—who licked his face and whined pleadingly. His Pack-Leader was not quite pleased with him, he could tell; but why did He make the ground heave this way? Barf was, he knew, going to be sick again at once.

Felicity, wrapped like a cocoon and snuggled in a sheltered spot on deck, grinned fiendishly even as she shivered. A sea gull perched companionably on the rail near her, making occasional comments and waiting to see if she'd produce something edible. Felicity regarded it with deep wonder. She'd never had any real contact with the animal world. In Virginia they'd had only horses and dogs, both of which had alarmed her back then. She'd changed a mite during the trip, she reckoned. She tried to imitate the gull's sounds, wondering what it was like to be a bird and to fly in the air, and what that very bright eye made of her.

She found out when she pulled out some leftover bread from breakfast and found it suddenly missing from her hand.

"He stole it!" she bleated so loudly that sailors came running. "He stole my bread!" she repeated accusingly; and then—grudging—had to laugh along with the men. Presently she began sharing her food, delighted when the gull, with several cousins, came to take it from her hand. Barf, too, between sessions of seasickness, seemed to decide that she was the female pack leader, and worth cultivating. He really was quite nice, she decided, letting him slurp his tongue all over her hand.

The ship headed north up a wild, splendidly beautiful coast of salt-and-pepper beaches, dark spiky firs and spruces, brooding rock faces and ice-white mountain peaks rising behind. She wished she could see more, but whenever she thought the sun was out for good, fog or clouds closed in, leaving the ship in shrouded mystery. Presently the north wind that had blown the rain clouds away, shifted west and blew them all back. It also caused the ship to toss in a manner that frightened most of the passengers, including Felicity.

"Do come down to the the cabin, honey!" pleaded Uncle Jon, who was looking oddly green. "Captain says we'll get no more sun now; it's going on November. You'll catch your death even if you don't fall overboard."

Felicity looked at him with scared eyes, but shook her head mutely. And before he could argue any more, Uncle Jon was forced to break off and rush over to the rail. Felicity looked at him and then Mr. Denny.

"It's the first time I've ever been healthier than somebody else," she observed with awe.

"Oh, the Northwest is healthy for Philo-Neptunians," he assured her. "Just ask Doc when next you see him. And never mind about missing the Mercer girls; they'll be there before you know it, and in the meantime you can make new friends. We've several young'uns. Laura Bell must be about your age. Ten or so?"

"Twelve," said Felicity with dignity. "You see," she informed him with morbid pride, "I had a Delicate Constitution even before the cholera."

Arthur Denny looked at her sharply and said no more.

Days later, there was more furious activity with sails and tiller, and now the ship turned eastward, to Felicity's surprise. Weren't they going to sail right into that rocky coast and have a wreck? But Mr. Denny explained that they were leaving the Pacific now, and heading for Puget Sound by a long water passage.

"This is the Strait of Juan de Fuca," he said. "It goes eastward for about ninety miles, between the Olympic Peninsula and Vancouver Island. Then we'll go south again, among all the islands of Puget Sound, for maybe sixty miles—and there we are."

"Who named all these places?" demanded Felicity.

"Some Spanish explorers named the Strait, and then an English captain did the rest. Vancouver, Puget Sound, Mount Baker, Mt. Rainier, Vashon Island—all for British naval officers."

"I'm surprised he could see anything to name," observed Arne looking around at the fog closing in again. "What with this and rain—Hope the captain knows where he's going."

Felicity did, too. Big swells were following the ship, rising from the west like smooth shadows and then vanishing ahead. The mist brightened before them—and then abruptly, as though passing through a curtain, they were in azure water and pale sunlight. Ahead and to the right, deeply forested hills piled higher and higher until they became white-topped mountains. One snowy peak to the south rose above all the rest.

"Mount Olympus," said Mr. Danny as the others caught their breaths. "Thank goodness Vancouver had the sense not to name that after some Admiral Littlewit or Captain Nettlebed or something."

They stared. "The Promised Land!" gloated Uncle Jon, thinking of Milk and Honey. Felicity stubbornly clung to her Virginian mansion in the forest. Arne had no such illusions. Now that Barf had got his sea-legs, Arne had time to observe the Dare's dreamy expectancy all through the strait, even when the wind shifted again and began driving masses of businesslike clouds and rain before it. South and south, between islands and points and bays, all the beaches piled high at the back with huge weathered gray logs. And at last they all stood eagerly at the rail watching the left shore, nearly there.

On a high bluff grew graceful dark-leaved trees which made Felicity's eyes widen.. "They look like magnolias!"

Denny shook his tawny head. "Madrona," he said. "But the leaves do look like magnolia; you aren't the first to think so. In fact, we call it Magnolia Bluff. Keep watching that shore, now," he added as the ship rounded the high wooded bluff end entered a large bay. "And there we are!"

Felicity looked.

"There, across the bay."

She looked again. No city. No stretches of velvet lawn. Not even half a colonial house without white pillers. Nothing but a sea of trees on piles of hills. Steep hills that ended abruptly in bluffs overhanging silver-sanded beaches with more of the silver-gray logs massed above the high-tide line. Forest that grew right to the edge of the bluffs, some trees leaning precariously over in apparent eagerness to join their brothers below. To the south, with great reluctance, the land sloped downward to sea level, making a flat sandy point and a small island. Felicity could make out a small clearing and a log cabin, and several figures who seemed to be waving and shouting. Was it a joke? It must be! She stole a look at Mr. Denny, but he was staring shoreward with the proud air of a new father. It wasn't a joke! Her lip began to quiver.

Arne had been expecting it. Her astonishing transformation aboard the ship had been a major miracle, certainly too good to last.

"Here we go again," he said resignedly. "What did you expect, Dollbaby, Williamsburg?"

The lip stopped quivering and reared itself outward. "I expected something!" wailed poor Felicity. "I had a right to expect something! And," she pointed out bitterly, "there isn't anything!"

Jon, too, was looking dismayed. But Arthur turned to Felicity with a rueful twinkle in his hazel eyes. "Oh, there's something there," he protested. "There's eight houses and plans for more. You can even," he added brightly, "see two of them from here. Look, way over on the left, on top of the bluff. That's Bell's new place. You folks may be staying in the old one for a bit. And right over there, at the Point; see? That's Doc Maynard's. It has two stories: bottom half, general store, and upper half where he lives. The Indians call it Makook House, which means 'Sell House' in Chinook."

Felicity stared. "It's nothing but a log cabin," she pointed out, aggrieved. "Is our house a log cabin too?"

"Not exactly," drawled Arne, his wide mouth curling upward in mischief. "Our house is still growing. We have to chop it down and turn it into one room, dirt floor, and holes for windows."

The half colonial house vanished forever. Feliciy's small nose quivered with outrage. "It just isn't decent!" she gasped. "It isn't decent for gentlefolk to live in places like that! Why, Uncle Jonathan, we'd never dream of putting our slaves in quarters like that, you know right well we wouldn't!"

Jonathan pulled himself together. "Certainly not!" he agreed with a firmness unusual for him. "And quite right." But Felicity's indignant brown eyes were demanding an explanation. "Slaves have no choice," he reminded her. "They didn't ask to be slaves, so we're obliged to do our best for them. But we are free, so if we want to live in log cabins, it's our own choice."

His niece looked at him, woeful and accusing. "It's not my choice!" she pointed out.. "I never wanted to come. I wanted to stay home in Virginia. But nobody asked me."

Arne, wishing to goodness she had stayed home, broke into a cheerful whistle which caused the fully-recovered Barf to start bouncing like a playful and overgrown ball. Mr. Denny smiled at Felicity sympathetically. "You know," he remarked, "it can't possibly turn out any worse than it seems to you now, and it might be a good deal better."

Felicity doubted it.

"Well, here's the Big City, folks!" roared Captain Johnson, red-faced with amusement. "Doc Maynard says it's going to be the Boston of the Northwest, but it don't look much like it now, does it?" And he gave Jonathan a final knee-buckling clap on the shoulder.

"Not much," agreed Jon feebly, rubbing the afflicted place. Felicity scowled at the offending captain (who remained blissfully unaware of her sudden hatred) and then at the shore. People were running down to the beach and pointing at the ship. They seemed to be mostly Indians. A sea-gull, circling overhead, gave a sharp shrill cry that sounded to Felicity like one of Arnes's jeers of derision. "Oh, hush your mouth!" she muttered, glaring at it. The gull, offended, flew away.

The clouds thickened. Again. By the time the baggage had been rowed ashore, they were clearly getting themselves in the mood for a steady attack. Felicity sat on the edge of one of the trunks and stared bleakly around. Mr. Denny was joyously greeting half a dozen grown-ups, two small girls and a baby, and introducing them to Uncle Jon. All of them, as far as she could tell, seemed to be named Denny, Bowen or Louisa, or perhaps all three. It was hard to hear, because not only were they all talking at once, but so were the dozens of Indians that crowded around—and not even in English.

At last someone noticed her, sitting forlornly alone. "We're so glad to have you!" smiled a vivacious dark-haired young lady, working her way through to Felicity. "I'm Arthur's wife, Mary Ann, and that's my sister Louisa, who is engaged to Arthur's brother David, and my daughters Louisa Catherine and Margaret Lenora, and now you're thoroughly confused, aren't you?" She smiled again. "Never mind, there's only a dozen of us so far, and another dozen young'uns; you'll have us straight in no time. Why don't you just sit here for a bit longer while we get the Indians out of Doc's house? I think your menfolk can stay there until we ready the old Bell place, but Arthur and I think you'd be more comfortable in with us, at least for a little while, and when Doc and your Mr. Mercer arrive, we can rearrange if necessary. Would that suit you?"

Felicity, flattered at being for just once in her life consulted, considered the matter of being separated from her uncle, and then, rather to her own surprise, nodded. Then, huddled in the rain which everyone else seemed to ignore, she watched Mr. Denny suggest to the Indians in that strange jargon Mrs. Denny called Chinook that they help carry things up the hill.

The Indians were smiling and friendly but not beautiful to settlers' eyes, being mostly short and squat, with foreheads that had been bound in babyhood so that they sloped sharply backward. They wore skins and blankets, long hair, and good-natured grins. The fleeting possibility crossed Felicity's mind that perhaps they considered themselves beautiful and the Whites odd looking?

"Klahowyah, tenas klootchman," squeaked a small boy, coming close to peer at Felicity with deep interest. Cocking his black head to one side, he gave her a gap-toothed grin, picked up a sort of necklace hanging about his neck, and held it out to Felicity, who blinked. "Tickey muck-a-muck?" he suggested, then ate one of the shriveled gray beads off it, smacked his lips, and offered it again. "Hiyu klosh," he urged encouragingly.

This was pushing hospitality a good deal too rapidly for Felicity. Besides, her young admirer was distinctly dirty and odorous, and she didn't even know what he was saying. She shrank back on her trunk.

"That's just Insaquecibut," said a husky voice behind her that materialized into Louisa, dark-haired like her sister, but shorter and plumper. "He's our pet imp. He's welcoming you, offering you dried clams, telling you that they're hiyu klosh, much good." The little fellow split his cheeks with a delighted grin, proffered the clams again. "They are, too, but not very clean in this case." And she smiled so warmly that Felicity forgot her woes for a moment.

"Oh," she said, and looked at the small face before her: round, brown, dirty, but so trustingly affable he reminded her of Barf. "Insa—" She stumbled on the complicated name.

"Insaquecibut. We call him 'Bit' for short," chuckled Louisa.

"Bit. Me Felicity," she ventured, pointing to herself.

Bit frowned. He smiled. "Flit!" he crowed, triumphant. "Flit, Bit, klosh tillicums!" He gave her a radiant grin and then dashed away, overcome by sudden shyness.

"Good friends," translated Louisa, and hurried off to help with one of the boxes. Felicity received the information and her new name a trifle dubiously. Mama would have had conniptions. Mama would doubtless have had conniptions at everything about this place. Mama would have cosseted her and demanded to go back to Virginia. The rain dumped itself with sudden ferocity. Felicity, wet in an instant, sneezed, shivered and agreed with Mama. She doubted she would live through it at all, or even wanted to …

"Holy Moses!" muttered Arne under his breath a few minutes later as a limp and faintly whimpering Felicity was borne tenderly up the path to the Denny cabin. Why, he wondered for the hundredth time, did people like that ever try to come West? Even Uncle Jon, nice as he was, was totally unsuited to be a pioneer. Felicity's parents had been hopeless, besides thinking they knew more about drinking river water than did Mr. Mercer. And as for Felicity—

Words and even thoughts failed him. He roughed up the sodden but delighted Barf—no, King!—and hoped passionately that Uncle Jon's wife and children, when they arrived, would turn out at least slightly better—but he wasn't very optimistic. At least, he remembered thankfully, the older one was a boy. Arne had a very low opinion of girls. Give him a dog, any day.

"Even," he told Barf—King—severely, "one that disgraces me by getting sea-sick."

Barf, overjoyed at the flattering attention, leaped up and managed to get Arne full in the face with that incredibly long wet tongue.

"Yuck!" said Arne.

CHAPTER 4

▼

THE MOUNTAIN THAT WAS GOD

"Poor little Doll-baby!" crooned Arne maddeningly. "It's that delicate mind of yours." He shook his head sadly. "Bats in your attic."

Felicity stamped her foot and wished for the sort of vocabulary Mama had never permitted to sully her ears. "Ooh!" she raged inadequately. "Ooh! You just hush up, Arne Knudsen!" Arne just grinned and went on pulling on his well-worn boots. "I wish," she sputtered, "that you'd—you'd go—take a walk!" Arne lifted his left eyebrow, which was much more active than the right and probably indicated an untrustworthy character. "In the bay!" she added earnestly.

The dreadful boy just chuckled and shoved a knitted cap over his fair hair. Felicity seethed. Nothing she could say ever got under his skin the way his jabs did hers; not since her successful naming of Barf: her only triumph. It wasn't fair. And it wasn't fair that she had had to stay in Doc's dark cabin for more than a week, nursing a perfectly dreadful chill.

Doc and Mrs. Denny had had a fierce argument when he and Mr. Mercer arrived to find her ill. Mrs. Denny said no man could take proper care of a little girl, especially with all the work awaiting his return. And Doc had retorted that that was what doctors did, in case she hadn't heard. Felicity begged someone to save her from Galloping Consumption, and Uncle Jon had clinched it by catching cold, himself.

And so nothing had been done yet about finding claims for the newcomers. It was only today they were to go, escorted by Mr. Denny, out to the lake past the Bell claim. And Felicity was still sitting here, feeling merely well enough to be restless, but with nothing to do but undergo the friendly inspection of the Indians who hung around Makook House, fascinated by all the things Doc had for sale. Oh, she admitted reluctantly, there had been occasional visits from Mrs. Denny or Louisa ... and Arne, of course, who was worse than no one even when he brought Barf. She glared at him. "I'm bored," she muttered sulkily. "And I want to see our claim."

"What's all this?" It was Mr. Mercer, vigorous and eager. Behind him, Jon glanced questioningly at Arne.

He sighed elaborately. "The Delicate Constitution wants to come with us."

There was an astonished silence. They looked at Felicity, who stared back mutinously.

"Come with us?" echoed Jonathan, forgetting who had stayed on deck during the trip up.

"Out to the claim?" echoed Tom Mercer, who didn't know.

"With all the bears and cougars and wolves and skunks?" suggested Arne wickedly.

She tossed her brown plaits. "I'm not a scaredy-cat about animals," she discovered, rather to her own surprise. "And," she hissed, glaring at Arne, "I reckon I'm used to skunks by now."

Arne blinked. It was the second time she'd surprised him by a good counter. He decided it was an improvement over tears.

"But honey," protested Uncle Jon. "You can't walk all that way; you just haven't the stamina. It'll be miles. And even if it has stopped raining, the forest will be simply drenched. Won't it, Arthur?" Mr. Denny, just entering, nodded reluctantly.

"Felicity wilted. "Oh," she mourned, and turned her back on them. "I can't do anything," she mumbled to no one in particular as Arne and the men went out. "Horrid place," she added, climbing up to sit on the big molasses keg so that she could stare glumly out the small square patch of window. "Nobody even likes me," she sniffled, and at the moment, she hardly blamed them.

Arne had forgotten all about Felicity as he plunged through the soggy forest at Jon's heels and listened tolerantly to the enthusiasm of the men. They—and Doc, too—were wrapped up in dreams for the future. Arne (except for wishing Barf were old enough to come too) was matter-of-factly interested in the present.

"Look at all this lush growth!" came Mr. Mercer's joyous voice from ahead. Arne obeyed. He had no choice. His rifle was entangled in it.

"Grow wonderful crops, I expect," Uncle Jon agreed.

Arne grinned, causing the crease in his rain-wet cheek to dent inward like a long dimple. "Where?" he drawled. "Show me a square foot that isn't already occupied!" For Arne, son of a farmer, knew how hard it was to wrest crop land away from virgin forest. No, he thought, the future of this place lay in the lumber—giant fir trees, thick as the hair on Barf's back—and in the sea. Doc was on the right track there.

Absent-mindedly he grabbed at a bush of soft, innocent-looking maple-shaped leaves—and let out a yelp of pain. The undersides and stems of those deceitful leaves were a veritable pincushion of inch-long needles!

"Ow!" he yelled. "Holy Moses!" He stopped and sucked his wounded hand, glaring at the treacherous plants.

The men had whirled with rifles at the ready. Then Mr. Denny laughed and relaxed. "Only devil's club. Painful but harmless. Nettles, too," he added, jerking his own hand away from a tattered plant that had so far resisted the coming winter.

Arne grinned ruefully as they started out again, still sucking his abused hand. "Fine paradise of yours, Uncle Jon," he jibed, "with devil's club in it."

Jonathan just laughed, but Tom Mercer turned his bearded face for a retort. "But new spring nettles make delicious soup! And they tell me there's no serpents in this Eden. No poisonous ones, anyway." He looked inquiringly at Arthur Denny.

"True enough. Well, west of the Cascades, anyway. Just pretty little green striped garter snakes."

They went on, thoroughly soggy by now. The hill rose more and more steeply to the left; presently they glimpsed a slab of gray through the trees downhill on the right.

"That's Tenas Chuck, Little Water," said Arthur. "There's another huge lake further east called Hyas Chuck, Big Water. I reckon, Tom, it should be easy to find a claim to fit your dream: salt Puget Sound in one direction, fresh Tenas Chuck in the other."

Tom grinned hugely. "And a spot for you, Jon, right next to us. And then when the city grows this far out—"

Arne stopped listening when they started planning a canal from Tenas Chuck to the bay. He frankly doubted this would ever happen. Or not for a few centuries, anyhow. He trudged along behind them as they skirted the edge of the lake, his own mind westward. His claim, when he reached twenty-one, wouldn't be on a mere lake, but along as much of Puget Sound as he could possibly get. He and Barf would live where he could watch the tides and storms, go boating and fishing, have the spray forever in his face and the salt in his nose.

"—when I bring the girls up," Tom was saying.

Arne sighed. Four more girls! Just what the place needed! There were already too many of them, and the only boys were baby Roland Denny, and Arne. The nearest male to his age was David Denny, who was twenty. Arne liked him, but he had reached the age of idiocy and was in love with Louisa Boren. No, until Charles Dare arrived, Arne would have to depend on Indians for companionship; particularly Qualchan, a Suquamish boy of his own age. Already they were friends, even though Arne's Chinook was as limited as Qualchan's English.

"—don't you, Arne?" asked Uncle Jon.

"Huh?"

"Don't you think this would be a perfect place for our house?"

Arne looked around. A brook trickled through forest and thick underbrush eastward down to the lake, now blue-washed under a clearing sky. Across the lake, hills behind hills rose steeply to give a hazed glimpse of snowy mountains to eastward. The lake was conveniently near. And a lake was better than no water at all. He and Qulchan could build a canoe and keep it here.

"Fine," said Arne.

Felicity still sat on her molasses keg and brooded. She had really wanted to go out in that darkly exciting forest. Back in Virginia she had scarcely ever wanted to do anything, especially if it was hot—which was frequently. Playing the pianoforte, or embroidering or horseback riding had no charms for her. Anyway, Adelaide could do all those things far better than she, so what was the point? And though she loved to sing, somehow no one ever noticed, so she'd mostly just read or dreamed in the drowsy air of the veranda, dressed in a froth of pastel ruffles and white lace, with the long rag-curled ringlets down her shoulders slowly drooping straight in the damp heat. Arne had teased her about those curls at the start, but now he teased her about the skimpy braids. She frowned.

It wasn't fair.

The door opened and Doc stood silhouetted in the oblong of gray light. "All alone inside, Felicity?" He shook his head so that the steel-rimmed octagonal spectacles that usually rested on his forehead began slipping down to their intended place on his nose. "That won't do. Hasn't Laura Bell been over to see you yet? No? Well, why not run out and get some fresh air, anyway?"

"I wanted to go with Uncle Jon," Felicity explained, "but they wouldn't let me. They said it was too far and too wet. My Delicate Constitution," she reminded him with a kind of resentful pride.

Doc nodded gravely, rightly guessing that poor health had been her one talent, as it were: the only thing that made her special. Now she was torn between clinging to it, and finding it a distinct nuisance. He came over, felt her pulse and looked at her tongue in the white light of the window.

"A bit peaky still," he admitted. "But you know, Felicity, this climate works wonders for the health; did anyone tell you? You just need to give it a chance. Right now, I'd suggest a canoe ride with Chief Sealth and me—You aren't afraid of Indians, are you?"

He had touched a sore spot. "Just because I'm sickly, everyone things I'm a scaredy-cat too, and it hasn't anything to do with it, and I'm not!"

"I beg your pardon," said Doc humbly. "You're quite right, of course, and it was stupid of me not to realize it. Get your wraps on, then, and meet me out front."

Felicity climbed the wall ladder and popped through the square hole in the ceiling that led to the living quarters of Makook House. She felt vaguely pleased. Doc had spoken to her as respectfully as if she were a grown lady, and she was going in a canoe. Elated, she tied the strings of her cloak, pulled the hood over her head, and decided against a second warm shawl. It wasn't very cold out.

In the clearing outside Makook House, Doc stood talking to a stately, blanketed Indian. His broad forehead was unflattened, and gray unbraided hair fell loosely over massive shoulders. He stood like a king. Felicity hesitated at the door, both shy and wondering. So this was the Chief of the Suquamish and Doc's best friend. A great man, said Doc; good friend to the settlers—who nevertheless would not speak a word of Chinook or English even though he probably knew them perfectly well.

She had frowned in puzzlement at this information; then remembered. Chinook was just a made-up trade jargon, not a proper language. "Well what is his real language?"

"Most of the Indians around here speak Duwamish."

"Oh." Felicity had been glad to get that straight. Now she looked at him searchingly. Doc had called him great, and she had supposed he meant great in size, for one never thought of a savage Indian being great-like-George-Washington. And yet—well, he was a good six feet tall and stalwart—but there was something else. Doc turned and beckoned her over with a few guttural words of Duwamish to the Chief, and as Sealth's deep-set eyes met hers with kindly courtesy, Felicity know what Doc had meant. Nobility—Greatness of spirit—She didn't try to put it into words, but she recognized it. Instinctively she curtseyed.

"Chief Sealth-uh" she murmuered, trying to end it with a sort of grunt, as Doc had done.

Doc beamed. Chief Sealth grasped her thin hand warmly in his strong one. And Felicity sensed somehow that these two had opened their friendship to admit her. It was a lovely feeling. She gave them one of the rare smiles that quite irradiated her sallow face, and walked happily between them across the clearing and down the path to the beach.

The clouds were beginning to thin rapidly as they reached Sealth's canoe. Not one of the clumsy affairs of roughly hollowed-out logs that some of the Indians used, but slender and beautifully shaped: both ends curving to a peak, with enough room in the open center for four or five people. Felicity sat in the middle and gripped the sides with excitement as the graceful craft moved lightly out into the waves of the bay, obeying the Chief's skilled paddle as if by magic.

The water, faithfully echoing the clearing sky, was beginning to shimmer with a silvery blue. A gull wheeled and laughed overhead—possibly the same one who had been so rude to her the day they landed. Felicity raised forgiving eyes to the smooth wide-winged body hovering dark and silver against the sky—

She gasped.

To the southeast, looming high over the tops of the highest mountains and the tallest firs, hung a huge glowing cone of frosted pearl, rising from a misty blue haze like something from a fairy tale.

The men stopped paddling and stared too. "Mount Rainier," murmured Doc in the tones of someone who has seen the miracle many times but will never quite get used to it. He turned to look at Felicity's rapt face, and smiled understandingly. "The Indians call it Tacoma: 'The Mountain That was God,'" he said softly. "We settlers say 'The Mountain' as if it were the only one that ever existed, the way I understand the Scots call Ben Nevis 'The Ben'."

Felicity, who had never heard of Ben Nevis, ignored this. "The Mountain That was God," she whispered. Oh, yes! Not the God who had meanly created her plain and sickly and untalented and Adelaide's cousin, and then orphaned her, but some glorious and shining Intelligence that made her heart go winging upward, made her want to cry with wonder and magic and beauty ...

In that moment, in a canoe in the middle of Elliot Bay, Felicity had her first faint glimmering that there might be a God she could truly love, and that this place might, after all, turn out to be rather a special place to live.

CHAPTER 5

▼

KLOSH TILLICUM

A dreary day. Felicity found herself on the same molasses keg, looking out the same window at the same damp square of forest and bay, feeling if anything more depressed than ever. The trouble with moments of wild elation was that they didn't stay, and godlike mountains vanished again behind the clouds, and ordinary life seemed worse than ever, afterwards. This particular let-down had lasted for days now, with Sealth being as invisible as Mount Rainier; and Felicity so mopish that Arne suggested building her an infirmary with bars and chains in their new house. Even Jonathan was driven into murmuring that 'Felicity'—happiness—was a sadly inappropriate name for his woeful niece. Perhaps it should have been Dolores the sorrowful. And he had sighed.

Felicity sighed too, now, even more deeply, disliking herself as well as everything else—except perhaps Chief Sealth. And it was raining again, and she was more bored than ever, and it was all very well to want to cheer up, but that was rather like wanting to be over a head-cold. Doc had suggested yesterday that she could help a bit around the store, but she had been feeling poorly, and he hadn't made any suggestions since. It was almost as if he were just quietly watching and waiting for something—though Felicity couldn't imagine what.

Anything would be more interesting than this! Even a quarrel with Arne. But Arne was off as usual with his new friend Qualchan, and Uncle Jon and Mr. Mercer had left this morning to go all the way down to Oregon City to file their claims and send for Aunt Julia, and they wouldn't be back for weeks. Felicity thought of going to find little Louisa Boren—the small one, who was Mrs. Denny's daughter—but she was only eight or nine, and more interested in her own younger sister. Anyhow, it was raining, and their house was a quarter of a mile away through dripping woods.

A little earlier, Makook House had been filled with Indians, trading, chattering in Duwamish and Chinook, running up and down that fascinating ladder against the wall to poke their heads through and look at the 'house above store'. Now even they were gone, and Doc was busy with letters and accounts in the back corner that was his office. Felicity sighed again, more loudly. Doc looked up, pushed his spectacles back up on his forehead, and regarded her thoughtfully.

"How about running out for some fresh air?" he suggested.

Felicity looked at him. "It's raining."

"So it is," he returned cheerfully. "It often is. But this isn't even the wet kind." Felicity wrinkled her short nose and tilted a perplexed head at him. "Thing is," said Doc, "if you never go out in the rain, you'll grow roots indoors. We're on a west coast with a warm ocean current, just like Great Britain, so we've a similar climate: mild and damp. On the other hand, I understand you don't much like the heat, and you won't get much of it here. So—"

Felicity was guilty of Interrupting her Elder. "You said the rain wasn't wet!" she reminded him accusingly.

"That's right. Not today's kind, anyway. No, I'm not crazy; ask anyone. Better yet, go out and see for yourself." He pushed his glasses back down on his nose and bent over his work.

Dubious, Felicity put on her mantle, threw a woolly shawl over her head, and went to stand in the doorway. Now that she noticed, it did seem to be falling in a fine misty spray rather than in drops ... Perhaps one didn't catch one's death in an Oregon Territory spray? At least Doc seemed to think not, or he wouldn't send her out in it. And he should know. And outside was certainly less gloomy than in.

She went out. It smelled nice. Sort of a green-and-russet smell, of rain, and salt and fir and wet leaves. The wind soughed in a gentle whispering song through the tall treetops, and rain floated down to lie in tiny droplets on the outermost wooliness of her shawl, hardly seeming to touch it, not soaking in at all. So that was what Doc had meant!

The drenched grass and tangle of brambles at her feet was another matter. Felicity looked at it doubtfully, and then forgot it altogether, for a pair of bright eyes was regarding her from the vicinity of her ankle with fearless curiosity.

Back home, no one had much use for wild critters. At best they were varmints to be grudgingly tolerated; at worst, vermin to be exterminated. She had never thought much about it. Now she found herself enchanted. She didn't even know what the critter was. "Oh, you funny little thing," she whispered, slowly kneeling and bending closer. "Don't be afraid."

It clearly wasn't. Boldly it came nearer, giving her a clear view of a tiny squirrel-like creature with stripes down its back and tail. It sat up, looked at her hopefully, pawed at the edge of her mantle with tiny hand-like paws. Its expression reminded her faintly of that bandit seagull on the brig, but its face was much more charming.

Before the acquaintance could progress, a small human figure popped out of the woods on the far side of the clearing, and her little critter vanished. The human paused and then darted toward her with a familiar face-splitting grin. "Klahowya, Flit!" it beamed, dashing up and waving its necklace of dried clams. "Tickey hiyu klosh muck-a-muck?"

Felicity made a pretty good guess at the meaning and shook her head firmly. The little critter was definitely gone, and she heaved a rather cross sigh. Still, she couldn't help smiling at the round eager face with its flattened forehead. How she wished she could speak Chinook!

Another movement at the edge of the clearing turned out to be a slim Indian girl of about her own age and a sturdy, sandy-pigtailed girl of perhaps ten. "Hullo," called Sandy-pigtails. Her high shoes, plain pantalettes and flannel dress were distinctly damp, clear up to her jacket, but she didn't seem to notice. "I'm Laura Bell, and this is Satco," she announced. "We live 'way up the bay, a mile as the crow flies, Pa says, but more by the trail. I came to see you while you were sick, but Doc said you were sleeping. And then the baby wasn't well, so I had to stay and help Ma, but today she said to run over and make friends with you."

She paused, as if expecting Felicity to produce a handful of friendship from her pocket. Felicity, being unable to do any such thing, and not quite sure what was expected, just stared helplessly. Adelaide, of course, would have known how to be gracious and superior and ladylike all at the same time; but Felicity didn't, so she just stood looking rather sullen and feeling altogether at a loss. Satco hung her head and Laura began looking disgruntled. But being a young lady of great determination, she rallied and broke the uncomfortable silence.

"We weren't going to bring Bit," she confided mischievously, "but he came anyway. He's in love with you. He told Satco—she's his sister—that you have gold in your eyes. Let's see." And she peered inquiringly into Felicity's puzzled face. If there were any gold in her brown eyes, it was the first she'd heard of it.

Bit, knowing he was being discussed, grinned happily, shuffled his moccasined feet, and took a bite of clam necklace. "Nika klosh tillicum," he said around it. "Nika chako nesika tenas klootchman."

Laura and Satco giggled. "I good friend. I come see little woman," Laura translated.

Felicity was touched. It was nice to be admired, even if only by a dirty little Indian urchin of no more than six years. "How do you say 'thank you'?" she asked, forgetting embarrassment.

"Mahsie," Laura told her, and Felicity gravely repeated it to Bit, who shuffled his feet harder than ever and looked up at her adoringly. Felicity, quite melted by this, blinked. Slowly the corners of her mouth curled upward to reveal small white teeth, an incipient dimple, and a definite sparkle in her eyes. "There *are* gold flecks!" Laura discovered, and suddenly they were all giggling, all friends. As simple as that.

"I want to learn Chinook!" said Felicity suddenly. "D'you reckon you can you teach me? Is it hard?"

"Easy as pie," said Laura promptly. "That's why it got invented, so English and French and Indians could trade and things, so they made it as simple as they could. There's only few words, really, and you use them describingly. Like tenas is little, so morning is tenas sun, and girl is tenas kloochman—little woman. And chuck means water, so tenas chuck is the little lake and salt chuck is the sea and skookum chuck is strong water, which means—"

"River?" guessed Felicity, the tiny dent beside her mouth deepening. Laura nodded. Felicity, delighted with herself and everything else, burst into a new volley of giggles that would have made Arne and Uncle Jon stare. But Laura, who needed no excuse for laughter, joined in, and then Satco. Bit regarded them with kindly but puzzled male tolerance.

"You know," remarked Laura presently, "Doc Maynard's fixing to get married soon, to a lady in Olympia, so they ought to have Makook House to themselves after, so maybe you'd like to come live with us until your house gets built, and let the menfolk have our old place."

Felicity stared.

"Ma and Pa think it would be a good idea," Laura added. "They said with four girls already, one more won't even be noticed, and everyone says you need young company." She ended with such a comical grown-up manner that Satco and Felicity giggled again.

"Did you come over today especially to ask me?" inquired Felicity, feeling quite flattered.

"Not exactly," Laura confessed with candor. "I wanted to find out whether I liked you. And at first I didn't think I would. You didn't seem very friendly. So I was just going to forget to mention it—coming to live with us, I mean. But then you turned out to be fun, after all, so I decided to remember."

"Oh," said Felicity a bit blankly. She wrinkled her brow slightly, decided that was more flattering than she had supposed, and then tucked a new idea into the back of her mind to think about later. It was smething to do with why people liked other people and why Arne didn't like her.

The thought of Arne gave her another new idea, and she turned to her new friends with a sudden bright glint in her eyes.

"Teach me some insults in Chinook!" she commanded.

CHAPTER 6

▼

FISH-FACE

"Thought you said it hardly ever snowed around here!" jibed Arne, wading through great heaps of it.

Qualchan turned a broad, good-natured face to glance back over his shoulder at Arne, and indicated that this was most unusual weather. David Denny grinned. "You must have brought it with you, Arne. Last year, we hardly had a dozen flakes."

There was a sound from above, and Qualchan yanked Arne foward just in time to escape the small avalanche of snow that an overburdened fir had deliberately flung at him. Unfortunately, it didn't miss Barf, and there was a muffled yelp from somewhere underneath. Arne hurled himself on it, dug frantically, and presently the patchwork pup emerged, torn between joy at being reunited with his Pack Leader, and reproach that He had played such a trick on him. His tail rotated madly, his erect ear lowered, he growled, whined and washed as much of Arne as he could reach. Then he indicated that he had had enough and would like to be carried, now. Qualchan grinned, David remarked that he had told Arne so, and Arne resignedly picked up the pup, who was at an extremely awkward stage of growth: too young to keep up in the snow but also too heavy to carry with any comfort whatever.

"I'll be glad when he gets his growth," panted Arne after a hundred yards.

David glanced back over his shoulder at the enormous paws dangling from the now-blissful puppy. "He's got considerable to go," he warned, and reverted to the original subject. "Anyhow, this snow is nothing compared to Illinois.".

Arne admitted it. "But back there we had towns and farms and roads, and could get supplies when we needed them," he gloomed, trying to remember how it felt not to be a little hungry.

David nodded seriously. Winter had produced storm after storm, and some eight inches of snow. Worse, no ships had appeared for weeks, and provisions were alarmingly low. No flour, or bread of any kind, even hardtack. Potatoes nearly gone. No milk or fruit or vegetables. Just game, fish, clams, tea—and wapatoes. Arne was duly grateful to the Indians for showing them where and how to dig those mealy, potato-like bulbs, but all the same, wapatoes weren't potatoes and never would be.

Oh well. It was undeniably a challenging life, and they wouldn't have changed it for worlds. They grinned cheerfully at one another, emerged from the woods, and started back across the clearing to Makook House. The path here was well trampled, so Arne thankfully put Barf down, and he scampered on ahead, ears flapping, to greet his lesser gods.

Doc and Chief Sealth stood out in front talking, with a well-bundled and mittened Felicity between them listening to the gutteral Duwamish as seriously as if she could understand a word of it. Doc spared her a smiling glance now and then, and the chief put his hand briefly on her shoulder as he planted his staff firmly in the snow to emphasize what he was saying. Felicity responded with one of her rare sunlight smiles, and Arne marvelled for the dozenth time at this astonishing friendship. Missy-Flissy, of all people! With an Indian! Who'd have thought it?

The conversation stopped as Barf arrived and began leaping up on all three of them (but mostly on Felicity, whom he adored second only to Pack Leader) with excited yelps of greeting. His ears and tail waved, his tongue was busy, he was enchanted to see her again. It was the one sign of idiocy the pup showed, and Arne, frowning, fervently hoped he'd come to sanity as he grew up. As the boys approached, Chief Sealth, always courteous, dropped his troubled air like a blanket and smiled at them. Then with a gracious gesture to Felicity, he turned down the slope toward the beach, Doc at his side.

Arne grinned derisively down at Felicity. "Look at Funny-face pretending she can understand Duwamish!" he bantered. Arne still hoped that if he went on teasing her long enough, some day she might learn to take it, and thereafter become human.

The day was evidently not yet. She turned a furious face to him. "Oh, sum-muckle, massachie komox!" she hissed, and turned her back so that he wouldn't see the tears. Funny-face! That was the awfullest name he had thought of yet! As if she could help her face! And it wasn't fair; she wasn't just pretending to understand Duwamish. She was learning it, helped by Doc, the Chief, Satco and Bit; and learning it very rapidly, too: they'd all said so. It was a pity she'd turned away, though, because she missed seeing Arne's shock and Qualchan's appreciative grin at her Chinook.

Fending off Barf, Arne hastily ran over his Chinook vocabulary. 'Shut up, wicked dog!' she had said! Felicity learning insults in Chinook! Probably especially for his benefit, too, he realized with some chagrin. Well, it was a change from crying, he decided, looking doubtfully at her back. He wasn't yet sure whether it was a change for the good or not, though Qualchan seemed to derive quite unnecessary amusement from it. Whose friend was he, anyway?

It was David who tactfully changed the subject. Sealth's canoe had shot out into the indigo waters of the bay. "What was the Chief looking so worried about?" he asked Felicity.

She stopped sulking and turned around. "He doesn't want us to name the town after him," she said, pointedly addressing David, not Arne.

"Why not?" asked David in surprise.

Felicity grew at least half an inch on the spot. Fancy her knowing something that older settlers didn't! "Well," she explained with overwhelming graciousness, "if anyone speaks an Indian's name after he's dead, it disturbs his spirit, and Chief Sealth is afraid he'd never have a moment's peace forever and ever. Doc's trying to persuade him that since we don't pronounce it properly anyway, his spirit needn't pay any attention. Nobody gets that funny grunt at the end, you know. Doc said we could change it even more and take out the grunt and change the T and L around so it would be Seattle. But the Chief isn't quite sure that would make any difference."

"But it's an honor!" protested Arne, not having noticed that Felicity wasn't speaking to him. "He—Hey, Doc," he called to the tall figure now reappearing from the beach. Are we going to be named New York Alki, after all?"

Doc shook his head so violently that his glasses fell down from his forehead and had to be pushed back. "Not even for my good friend Sealth!" he said grimly. "And it would be even worse than that. You know what name they're trying to stick us with? Duwamps, that's what! Look! Moxlie's Canoe Express finally got in with the mail, and it brought this!"

'This', which Doc held as if it were a nettle, was a letter addressed to Dr. David Maynard, Town of Duwamps, King County, care of Olympia, Oregon Territory. Arne and David stared with shocked faces while Felicity, feeling superior because she had already seen it, watched.

"Duwamps!" exclaimed David, finding that it tasted as nasty as it sounded. "Where did they get that?"

"Someone's version of Duwamish River, I guess," growled Doc, and glared at Arne. "And you'd better not laugh, m'boy. Your own future is involved. Can you imagine a place with the name of Duwamps ever becoming a great city?"

Arne couldn't imagine this bit of steep, wet, forested wilderness as a great city under any name, and he couldn't resist teasing Doc by saying as much. Doc's eyes snapped with indignation. "You have no imagination!" he accused Arne.

"Not that much," agreed the dreadful boy cheerfully, the crease deepening in his left cheek as he noticed Felicity glowering at him with that comical mis-matched frown. (He never dreamed that his own left eyebrow lifted independently of the right.) "Anyway, if the Head of the Territorry says we're Duwamps, how are you going to argue?"

"By my own authority, that's how." Doc waved a letter triumphantly. "This officially names me Justice of the Peace and Notary Public of this county, and my first official act will be to record this town as Seattle."

David suddenly lost interest in the name of the town. "Did you say Justice of the Peace?" he demanded eagerly.

Arne groaned. Doc chuckled. "You and Louisa have a job for me?" he suggested delicately. "Well, it'll take at least two or three weeks—more if it goes on snowing—to finish your cabin. By that time we'll have moved Felicity in with the Bells, and I'll canoe down to Olympia to get myself married to Catherine, and then by late January, say, come back and do the same for you."

Arne groaned again. "I don't know what gets into men!" he lamented. "No sooner do they grow up then they lose their minds and get married. To girls, too!" He shuddered.

Felicity bridled. David cuffed his ear with an insultingly older-brother air. "Callow youth," he drawled tolerantly. "Never mind, you'll outgrow it."

"I hope not!" Arne bleated in alarm, and Felicity beamed at seeing her arch-enemy, for once, on the defensive.

David grinned at her. Give him three or four years at most," he predicted. "When he starts proposing to you, Felicity, make it hard on him. Make him get down on his knees and beg."

They both indicated utter nausea at the idea, but Arne got off the first shot.

"Ugh! Anyone but Fish-face! I thought you were my friend, David!"

Felicity turned and stalked into Makook House, heart pounding with outrage, fighting back hurt tears. She had taken enough from Arne Knudsen! He was always sneering at her, always saying the thing that would hurt most. And the others didn't care; they just thought she was a baby about being teased. Well, if she'd had Adelaide's looks, she could have laughed at Arne's insults. But his insults were very near the truth, and it was hard to take teasing that hurt.

Inside, she hesitated a moment and then climbed the ladder to the upper story. She'd get her things packed right now and move to the Bells' as soon as they'd let her. She couldn't get away from Arne fast enough.

Funny-face! Fish-face! Broodingly, she picked up the tiny hand mirror and went over to the small window with it. Her own face frowned back at her, dim in the light permitted by oiled paper; but she could see enough. Too much. It certainly wasn't much of a face. Thin and pointed, it was, with shadows at the temples and under the cheekbones. (Adelaide's was full and dimpled.) There was a great deal of forehead, which Mama always said was a sign of nobility and intelligence—but Felicity had her doubts about this. She felt that she could easily have done with less forehead—especially since the nobility and intelligence were far less in evidence than the oddity of her frown, which she was noticing for the first time. No wonder it never impressed anyone much! It was a pathetic mis-matched thing, one eyebrow flat across the top and the other scrambling itself over her nose—not at all like Arne's elegantly derisive lifted brow. And the rest wasn't much better. Wistful brown deer-eyes. (Adelaide's were blue.) Pallid skin. (Adelaide's skin was magnolia white, her cheeks rose-pink.) A pale drooping mouth. (Adelaide's was full and red.)

Mama used to say Felicity had good bones, so she stared at the bones for some time, without much enthusiasm. They certainly were very visible, but not, she decided, beautiful. And the whole discouraging blob of nothing was framed in that fine dull-brown hair pulled straight back and braided into long limp plaits falling on both sides of her skinny neck, looking even worse than the old rag-curls. Ooh! No wonder Arne made nasty remarks! She didn't like her face any better than he did: less, because she was the one who had to wear it—but he needn't be cruel about it, all the same. She really hated him for it.

Quite suddenly, and with no one around to appreciate it, Felicity had herself a private little tantrum. She sobbed. She threw things (but not breakable ones). She stamped. She didn't feel a bit better. She pulled her own hair. It hurt—and it also gave her an idea.

Doc's large shears were on the top of a packing case. Felicity lifted them, hefted them, opened and shut them a few times. And then, deliberately and with a good deal of malice, she cut off her braids. The sound and feel of shears crunching through hair was grimly satisfying, and so was the oddly light, loose sensation when she shook her head. Pleased, she went on cutting., When Doc came in a few minutes later, it was to see a jaggedly crop-haired small person staring at him defiantly from the one real chair in the room.

"I cut it off," she announced unnecessarily. "I was plumb mad, and I still am, and I don't care! I reckoned I couldn't possibly look any worse than I did, but if I could, I would." Her lip quivered, but no tears fell.

Doc blinked, recovered from his shock and, and understood a good deal that he hadn't before. "Well," he observed casually, "you do believe in doing things well, don't you?" He grinned conspiratorially and Felicity was surprised into a wavering smile. "Let's see what you've done here," he went on, taking off his jacket and coming over to her. "Mmm." He tilted her head this way and that, studying it judiciously.

It wasn't at all the sort of reaction Felicity had expected. All the defiance drained out of her, and she found herself waiting nervously for his judgement.

"You know," he said thoughtfully, "I believe it's going to suit you. Here, come down to the kitchen; I've hot water on, and we'll wash it. Only first, let me do a bit of shaping here and there. Actually, you didn't do at all badly, considering your state of mind, but I think it should be—oh, say—two inches all over? Here, give me those."

Bemused, Felicity gave him a small smile along with the shears. Somehow her act of rebellion had become a shared adventure, though she wasn't quite sure how. Spirits lifted, she submitted, while Doc studied and clipped and shampooed. How light it felt! How easy to wash and dry! And with the old dry ends gone, it was soft and silky as a baby's.

"Mmm, nice," grunted Doc, rubbing it dry beside the roaring fire. "This is wonderful water, isn't it? Pure as snow. Believe you're going to have just a bit of curl," he added, his hands busy with comb and hair. "It's turning up in a perky little duck tail here at the nape of your neck."

He held her off at arm's length, regarding her with smug satisfaction. You know, I think I missed my profession. Should have been a ladies' hairdresser."

Felicity giggled.

"Don't laugh at me, Miss Pixie," he said with mock severity. "Here, take a look at yourself."

Felicity looked. Her eyes widened. Was it possible? That high forehead was half hidden under a slightly waving fringe of hair, ruddy in the firelight, feathering across to cluster gently around her temples. The hollows and angles and sharp bones were softened, giving her face a faintly elfin air, and her eyes looked dark and luminous.

She raised them wonderingly to Doc. "Great day in the morning!" she breathed. "Doc, I'm—that is—Don't you think I look—well—almost pretty? Not really pretty, of course," she amended hastily. "Not a bit like my cousin. But much nicer than before. And my neck doesn't look so skinny, either," she gloated.

I don't know your cousin," said Doc gravely, "But I know a very pretty face when I see one. Yours reminds me of a wildflower—perhaps a trillium—set on that slender little neck. Felicity, my dear, has no one ever told you that you'll be a very lovely girl one of these days?"

No one ever had. Felicity found it a little hard to believe, but she smiled radiantly at her reflection and then up at Doc.

Terribly pleased with themselves, they solemnly shook hands.

CHAPTER 7

▼

EYES IN A BUSH

"Last one down to the beach is a skunk!" shrilled Olive Bell, and hurled her small self over the top of the bluff, Satco and Bit directly behind.

Laura paused to give little Virginia a hand, and to glance half apologetically at Felicity. "You'd better not try it again, Flit. We'll be back up soon." And she followed the others.

Felicity stood on the edge and watched them tumbling down the steep slope to the pewter-gray logs and sand below. It looked fun. It was fun. She had tried it once, when the snow had all melted right after she moved in with the Bells. Only, having got her down, her muscles had flatly refused to get her back up again, and the others had had an awful time pushing and pulling before they finally hauled her up, panting and half tearful, back over the top of the bluff where the Bell cabin stood. And since then she had felt horribly out of things. Gloomily she turned her back to Puget Sound. Might as well go inside, where at least there was Mrs. Bell to talk to and the baby to play with.

She had hardly taken a reluctant stop when a motion in the bush just ahead stopped her. Another wild critter? She tilted her head and waited, realizing that she truly liked animals, even the wild kind. Perhaps it was another little stripy one, like that other time. When she had described the friendly little critter she'd seen, they all said tolerantly that it sounded like a chipmunk, but didn't they hibernate? Or did they? Anyway, she must surely know what chipmunks looked like?

Felicity had hung her head, cast a sideways look at Arne all ready to jeer at her, and refused to defend herself. How could she know what any animals looked like, except the carriage horses and hunting dogs, when she'd been carefully kept from them? Might catch lockjaw, said Papa. Ladies didn't spoil their hands and complexions outside except for Riding, said Adelaide. All critters were Filthy, said Mama.

But her family were not here, and this pair of eyes was. Felicity stood quite still, trying to make out what kind of critter it might be. The eyes in the shadows were a lot larger than the chipmunk's. She carefully squatted, regardless of her blue skirt on the damp ground, and stared.

The shape backed deeper into the bush, clearly uneasy. It occurred to Felicity that she herself found a hard stare from human eyes to be quite unnerving, so maybe—She lowered her gaze a bit and began crooning softly. "Hello? Who are you? A rabbit? I won't hurt you."

"Meow," said the rabbit fretfully, and inched forward. Now Felicity could just glimpse a small head, white paws and large pointed ears.

"My stars!" she murmered. "Are you really a cat? A wild one or a tame one? And if you're tame, where do you belong, and what are you doing here? Come on, love, let me see you."

"Eew?" it said plaintively, and stayed firmly where it was. It looked horribly thin, not to mention wet and cold. Felicity had never been on so much as speaking acquaintance with a cat (Filthy and dangerous) but her heart went out to this one.

"Come here, then, and I'll help you." She stretched out her hand, slowly and carefully—and instantly the lean shape streaked away into the woods. Felicity straightened, dreadfully disappointed, and gloomed her way to the house. What had she done wrong?

Mrs. Bell looked up from her sewing, fair hair a smooth cap plaited around her head. "Hello, dear. Cold? Oh, your dress is damp. Wrap that blanket around you and come to the fire."

Felicity obeyed. "Mrs. Bell, have you got a cat?"

It was a silly question; she'd have seen it by now, wouldn't she? But Mrs. Bell raised an interested head. "Not really. But sometimes we've thought we heard a cat crying near-by. Why; have you heard it, too?"

"I just saw it. It's spotty I think, with white feet, and so thin and wet and cold! But it ran away before I could help it."

"Mmm. I wonder. Seems to me one of the ships lost their cat while it was in here, some months ago. Could have taken to the wild and survived, I reckon. Poor thing! Would you like to put out food for it, Felicity?"

Felicity raised an eager head. "Could I? Can we spare it?"

"Meat, we can always spare," said Mrs. Bell wryly. "Get a bit from the larder, if you like, and put it out. And when you come back, maybe you could keep an eye on Lavinia for me for a bit? She's into everything lately, and I would like to finish this dress for Olive before it's time to start dinner."

Felicity pulled the youngest Bell daughter away from the dogfish-oil lamp in the nick of time, and went to the larder. It held only meat, but plenty of that. She took a small bit of yesterday's venison, and went back out to the empty bush where she'd seen the cat.

"Hello?" she called softly. "Little kitty, are you hungry?" There was no sound or movement; with a sigh she put the offering where the cat had been and went back in. "What's for dinner?" she asked without much hope.

Mrs. Bell smiled ruefully. "Guess."

Felicity sighed. Clam soup, venison, and—duck?"

"Quail this time." Mrs. Bell held up Laura's maroon flannel dress which she was re-making for Olive. "And wapatoes, too, if Arne brings some by. Stir the soup for me, will you, dear?"

Felicity obeyed, glancing at the dress as she did so. It was almost worn out, but Olive was lucky to get even hand-me-downs these days, what with many folk reduced to flour-sacking and buckskin until a ship should arrive. Felicity thought guiltily of her own two almost-new dresses.

"Couldn't Laura wear one of my frocks?" she suggested, feeling even guiltier for not having thought of it sooner. "She's only a bit shorter and wider than I am—" Her voice trailed away. She wanted to say that she knew she was a nuisance, a seventh person to feed and to crowd into the cabin, and a sickly, useless person, at that. She couldn't cook or do the practical things that Laura did, and even her sewing wasn't as good as it might be. In fact, her domestic skills were about that of six-year-old Olive: stirring soup, setting the table, and drying dishes. She was only just realizing how dreadfully no-count she was, but to say it out loud would somehow make it more true.

"Reckon I just wasn't cut out to be a pioneer," she mumbled, pulling Lavinia back from the tempting fireplace.

Mrs. Bell bit off a thread. "That's what they said about me," she returned cheerfully. "and look how wrong they were. What a help it is to have you watch

Vinnie," she added, and Felicity felt a little better. But she did wish Uncle Jon would get back from Oregon City—

Arne, trudging northward up the muddy trail which bore the optimistic name of Front Street, paused to shift the sack of wapatoes from one shoulder to the other and take a firmer grip on his rifle. Front Street! he thought with a grin. And this little cross street just ahead was James Street, even though there was nothing on it but the beginnings of Mr. Yesler's lumber mill. And where James Street ran down the hill to the beach, there would be a wharf for loading the lumber. Big dreams for a small scratch in the wilderness—but Arne was beginning to believe it. These dreamers were so energetic, so sure of themselves and the future greatness of Seattle!

He paused for a moment to contemplate. Barf, supposing the journey to be over, tried to throw himself into his Pack-leader's arms. He was considerably larger and heavier than he'd been in October. Arne clutched, sidestepped, tried to duck the sodden cedar branch hanging across the path, and didn't duck quite far enough. It poured cold water down his neck.

"Yowp!" said Arne, and stepped off the path. A thorn promptly attacked him between the top of his boot and his too-short trouser leg. Barf, thinking it a new game, grabbed the trouser leg in his teeth and tried to pull it off.

Arne used two or three quite new words he'd picked up from one of the deck-hands on the way up, smacked Barf (but not very hard), and concentrated on mastering both the path and his disreputable giant of a puppy all the way up to Bell's clearing. Then he paused at the top of the bluff to stare for a moment out across the bay .

Puget Sound had suddenly become very calm, and the low winter sun, shafting through a hole in the clouds, turned it to liquid golden light. Above, the gulls, complaining loudly, cut bright spirals in the air. Far westward across the Sound, the snowy peaks of the Olympic Mountains began to etch themselves against the sky—and from across the bay something else was etching itself, rounding the northern point.

Arne gave a yell of delight and raced for the Bell cabin. "A ship!" he whooped. "Ship coming in! Hot biscuits tonight!"

With an answering whoop, half a dozen children shot up over the bluff and past Arne, racing back along the trail toward Makook House. Mrs. Bell appeared in the doorway, too late to call any of them back, her face a mixture of joy and indecision. And behind her, a blanket wrapped around thin shoulders, was Flit. "Wish I could go, too," she said wistfully.

"Oh no, you don't!" he retorted with a paternal authority that was totally insulting. "It was bad enough getting you up here in the first place, Fleecy; what do you think I am, a horse?"

Felicity stuck out her lower lip at him and wished for adequate words and huge muscles with which to toss him over the bluff.

"Oh dear!" murmured Mrs. Bell. "I do wish I could run down and get some supplies in time for dinner. But—" She hastily vanished back inside as an ominous crash annunced that Vinnie was into something.

Felicity opened her mouth. "I—"

Arne stopped her. "Look here, Missy Flissy," he hissed. "You offer to stay here and watch the baby while I go back with Mrs. Bell, hear me? It's the least you can do to make up for being so much trouble. I mean it!" he added threateningly as Felicity's lip shot out even further. "If you don't, I swear I'll—"

Her eyes blazed amber in a perfect fury of rage, frustration, and wounded dignity. "Oh!" she squealed. "Oh, you mind your own business, Arne Knudsen! I don't need you to tell me what to do! That's just what I was going to say, myself, and now you've gone and—Oh, I just hate you! I *was* going to!" she reiterated to his skeptical grin.

"Sure you were," he agreed engagingly, not believing it for a moment. "Just pretend I never said anything—but do it!"

Felicity shot him a glance of passionate dislike, and turned as Mrs. Bell emerged with her youngest, both liberally daubed with dogfish oil. "Mrs. Bell, you can go down; I'll clean Vinnie up and watch her."

Mrs. Bell looked relieved. "Would you mind, Felicity? Do you think you'll be all right?"

"Of course she will," said Arne firmly. "Bears are hibernating, wolves don't come this close in, and there's no livestock to attract cougars. There won't be any Indians come a-calling because they'll all be down at the ship, and anyway, Flit will be inside with the door bolted. Just you come along, Mrs. Bell, and don't let Barf climb you—Or if you'd rather," he added with great heroism, "I'll stay here, too—"

Mrs. Bell glanced at Felicity, who was clearly finding it quite impossible to put her feelings about Arne into words. "I think Felicity would rather you didn't," she observed mildly. "It's wonderful of you to offer to stay, dear. I'll just get my mantle."

Presently, with a warm smile, she was gone, her full blue skirts and mantle disappearing down the trail behind Arne and an excited plumy tail. The forest rustled faintly around the clearing, and a blue jay squawked from high in a giant

Douglas Fir—a tree so huge that she, Laura, Olive, Satco and Flit combined could barely get their arms around it. She hugged the slippery Vinnie to her, and moved gently over to the bush were the little cat had been. Nothing was there— not even the venison. Hopefully she staggered to the larder, withdrew some more venision, and then (still carrying the baby) went back outside. A furtive shadow—or shadows?—vanished into another bush, nearer the house.

"There, now!" Her soft caressing voice would have startled Arne. "Are there two of you? Who's a brave little kitty? Come along, then; I'll leave it right here for you." She did so, and moved backwards a few steps. A shadow moved a little but stayed firmly where it was.

Vinnie began to struggle. Felicity sighed, took her into the house and began the cleaning process. But though she moved softly and kept peeking out to look at the bushes, nothing happened and the meat stayed where it was. Disappointed, she took the now sleepy baby in her arms, sat in the precious rocker and brooded.

She was sick and tired of herself. Mama had always seemed vaguely proud of her daughter's delicacy, as a sign of sensitive and superior Blue Blood, as in The Princess and the Pea. Felicity had always privately thought it a great nonsense to suppose anyone, however sensitive, could feel a pea through twenty mattresses. Now she was also doubting the superiority of a delicate constitution. Of what possible use was it? Especially out here in the far West! It just kept her from doing anything enjoyable or interesting or useful, and it made Arne—and probably everyone else, too, however kind—loathe her for being a burden and a nuisance.

Vinnie, worn out with exploration, curled up on the bearskin rug and went to sleep. Felicity lifted her to the center of the big bed and then stood still for a minute, her eyebrows puckered mutinously and unevenly.

Who cared what that nasty Arne thought, anyway? But Felicity did, and she knew it. She cared even more what she herself thought, and this realization caused her to stamp her foot on the dirt floor. She clenched her fists. Then she went and stood in the open doorway and sniffled, while the irritated bluejay flew to a higher branch and then turned and scolded her.

Slowly the self-pitying droop of her mouth tightened to a rebellious line. She concentrated. And while Lavinia slept, and the rest of the town bought flour and potatoes and yard goods, and Mr. Yesler's lumber-mill machinery was slowly unloaded from the schooner and shadowy little cat forms crept ever so warily to get the new gift of meat, Felicity Ann Dare was making the most important resolve of her whole life.

CHAPTER 8

▼

MANY CHALLENGES

It is all very well to develop a sudden determination to become strong and healthy and useful—but how did one set about doing it? Felicity puzzled when she should have slept. And the next day, when Chief Sealth dropped by, she managed to get him alone for a bit. After all, he was strong as a fir. Standing in the drizzly rain in front of Bell's, she put her problem to him in her best Duwamish, liberally patched with Chinook and English when she ran out of words, in a way that set his deep-set black eyes twnkling under jutting brows.

Though he would never speak a word, himself, of anything but his own tongue, he was quite willing to listen to Felicity in any language. Now he gave her a pleased nod and proceeded to consider her problem with gratifying gravity. When he answered, it was in simple Duwamish.

"When you use your body more, it will grow stronger. But you need a strong spirit, too. Your spirit is you. What you think, that is you. Think strong, shining. Your body will answer to your thoughts." Felicity thanked him, wide-eyed, but sighed a little. It was too simple—and too hard. She didn't think she could do it. She didn't even know how to start.

A flicker of movement near the house caught her eye, and also, of course, that of the Indian. His keen glance swept a bush and returned to Felicity. "I think you have a little friend?"

"Oh, I wish it were true! It's so hungry and miserable! But it's scared of me."

Though he used some Duwamish words she did not know, Felicity nevertheless understood him to say that the little creature felt the shining thoughts in her spirit, and wanted very much to love and trust her; so she needed patience.

"Truly?" breathed Felicity, overwhelmed. Nobody—nothing—had ever wanted to love and trust her; not like this.

"Good start to your new trail," he said, warm approval on his face. "Go on, one foot and one foot." He turned and left, silently as was his way. She stared after him, not sure if she dared believe it. To be strong and useful, one must earn the love and trust of a cat? Well, she would certainly try, but perhaps she should try some other things, as well. Perhaps Doc could give her some medicine. She didn't even care if it was nasty, so long as it worked.

And in the meantime, it occurred to her—startlingly—that when Uncle Jon got back and they built and moved into their cabin, until Aunt Julia arrived, guess who would be the Woman of the House? A terrifying thought! And there were no slaves or servants, and Uncle Jon and Arne would be busy doing man's work, and anyway, Felicity would die before letting Arne cook for her. Great day in the morning! However would she manage?

Felicity began watching Mrs. Bell with the fierce concentration of a kitten having its first mousing lessons. She watched the roasting of meat, the use of the Dutch oven, the baking of bread and biscuits, and pies both of game and of last year's dried berries. She took note of the things to be done with clams, fish, wild fowl, venison and rabbit, not to mention potatoes and wapatoes. While all the men and many of the Indians worked at setting up Mr. Yesler's lumber mill, while rain fell with quiet determination from a dreary sky, while the other children played outside anyway and throve on it, Felicity stared at Mrs. Bell's capable hands.

She asked questions. Why do you squish the bread down again after it rises? How do you know when the Dutch oven is hot enough or when something is done? What would happen if you didn't make slits in the top of the pie crust? Mrs. Bell not only answered and explained, she showed Felicity how to do things, then let her help, even with the difficult bits. And she seemed to understand without being told that it was a secret. Especially from Arne.

There were unexpected complications, like arranging it so that everything was ready to eat at the same time. The first time she cooked an entire meal, the hoecakes were burned and the rabbit half raw, and she nearly cried of humiliation. And more than once she forgot something important like salt; and her first fritters crumbled to bits before they were half cooked; and now and then a dish turned out to be altogether different from one she had intended. But Mrs. Bell said she was learning remarkably quickly, Olive and Virginia and Mr. Bell quite liked whatever it was that the salt rising bread had become, and Laura remarked half enviously that Flit's sourdough bread was better than her own.

During this time she wooed the shadow (shadows?) assiduously. Morning and evening she went out with a little offering of meat or fish, and presently they began to wait for her, as if they had their own private clocks. She usually knelt near the food, coaxing the little things to come out. But the glowing eyes always stayed decidedly where they were. Then one day she was greeted by a piercing little voice screeching that she was Late (which was true) and should be Ashamed of Herself.

Felicity set the food down and sat back on her heels, round-eyed while a tiny head appeared from within the bush and poised there, still shouting. It was the first good look Felicity had had, and she stared, entranced, at the vivid pattern on the little creature: wild swirls of gold, copper, bronze, cream and apricot on a mostly-mahogany body. It returned the stare for a moment and then delivered another speech, long and impassioned, about Starving to Death, and Not One Step Nearer or Mama would Get Her.

Mama, thus appealed to, appeared and swept her baby back with a paw and a growl. She was another beauty, was Mama, with vividly blotched black and orange head, tail and body, white chest and legs, and a sweetly pretty white face, with black and orange swirling across golden eyes—quite out of character with the threats she was making. She regarded Felicity fiercely—not only growling like a dog, but spitting—and definitely declining to come closer. Not even for food, she hissed. Or her children, either, she added pointedly.

Felicity sighed with delight and frustration, but the next day. they were waiting again, and more visibly. Mum sat boldly in full sight, with the swirled beauty at her flank shouting Here She Was, and Hurry Up with the Food. Something white and gold peered out and yawned, while a white muzzle against a tawny shadow lurked just behind. Mama crept forward, flat to the ground, ears back, growling like Barf, until she could snatch the meat and bolt back into the bush, where Felicity, peering, could make out four probable shapes and a lot of satisfied gobbling.

"That'll be mother and kittens, all right," said Uncle Jon when he managed to catch a glimpse of them. He knew a lot about cats, it turned out. "Must be the ship's cat they mentioned; came ashore to have her litter, I reckon. I'd say they're about five months old now. Amazing that any of them survived!"

Mrs Bell nodded. "Tell you what, Felicity, you go on trying, especially with the mother: she's used to humans. We could use a good mouser."

By the time of David and Louisa's wedding, Felicity had managed a good look at all four. The mother cat (whom she named Marilla for her grandmother who had been a scolding beauty) was the boldest, snatching food from her hand, and occasionally tolerating a fleeting caress as she departed. The gold-and-white was the first kitten she actually touched—briefly—and only because it was too lazy to move away from her hesitant finger. Easy-going to the point of folly, it would just lie there—out of reach, to be sure—but relaxed and insouciant, waiting for food to arrive—at which point it became just as lively as the others.

The third kitten was still mainly a lurking shadow with white muzzle, and glowing greenish eyes, staring at her unblinking. Shadow would be a good name for it.

But the tapestried talker was her favorite, and an imp of Satan if she ever saw one, alternatively flirting, scolding, preening; once actually letting Felicity get almost near enough to touch, and then swatting and dancing away. It also invariably—and often successfully—tried to get the lion's share of the food from its larger siblings and even its mother.

"The thing is," she explained to Uncle Jon when the menfolk came by on their way to cabin-building, "The gold one's so sweet and gentle it must be a girl, but that littlest one is so beautiful it ought to be, too; so I suppose Shadow must be a boy. He's provoking enough."

Arne blinked and tried to decide if it was a deliberate insult. Uncle Jon shook his head. "You can't tell much by their looks or personalities," he told her. "But the larger ones are likely to be male, especially the gold and white; they usually are, for some reason. And Marilla and your little tapestry are certainly females."

"How do you know?

"If their coloring has both orange and black, they always are."

"Why?"

"I don't know: they just are."

"Oh." She pondered it, while Arne stared at Uncle Jon, definitely impressed by such arcane knowledge. "What's a tapestry?"

"A beautiful bit of woven pattern, like her coat, only usually telling something."

Felicity rubbed the place on her wrist where a patterned paw had told her something, all right. "That's her," she said ruefully. "Pest for short! Now, how about the yellow one?"

Arne, still smarting about poor Barf's name, tried for a bit of revenge."

Daffodil?"

She whirled to stare at him. Arne, expecting outrage, disappointingly got delight. "Oh, yes; that's funny! We could call him Daffy for short. Sometimes you do have good ideas, Arne. Not very often," she added, mercifully failing to notice his chagrin, "but now and then. Now all I have to do is tame them." She sighed happily, and thereafter redoubled her efforts.

Early in February, Uncle Jon arrived back on the brig Samuel Adams without Mr. Mercer, who had decided to stay on in Salem with his daughters until spring.

"His friends there wanted to adopt the girls," Uncle Jon reported, "But Mary Jane hit the ceiling. Said they were a family and would stay together no matter where. I think the Hortons and young Becky are coming back with them, so that's another family for Seattle."

"Great!" muttered Arne. "Five more girls is just what we need!"

Felicity stuck out her tongue at him, and Jonathan noticed vaguely that she seemed a mite more perky than before, and not quite so quick to cry. He still supposed she and Arne secretly enjoyed bantering each other. Probably he was about half right. Felicity watched them head back to town. The Bell house seemed a long way out—but not as far as the Dare house would be. Two or three miles from Makook House, Arne had observed, and wasn't Flissy going to be scared way off there in the wilderness? Uncle Jon added encouragingly that they'd only be quarter of a mile or so from the Mercers, once theirs was built, and with a nice wide trail between them. Since it was totally useless trying to make either of them believe she wasn't a scare-baby, she just said something excessively rude in Duwamish (which neither could understand) and left it at that.

Actually, she was not at all nervous about the forest. When she wasn't coaxing cats or learning to housekeep, she wandered in the woods, loving them more and more; discovering that she had some sort of inside compass (like the cats' inside clocks?) and no matter how she zigged or zagged in her wandering, she always knew her way back without thinking. (Arne, who got lost if he so much as turned his head, didn't believe this, but Uncle Jon did. "Oh, yes, it runs in the family. I've a perfect sense of direction, too." he said matter-of-factly, while Felicity smirked at her enemy.) She listened to the sounds of animals and birds, and in the evenings picked Mr. Bell's brain for all his woodcraft lore.

Once she heard a blood-curdling call that began at the lowest sound of her perception and rose eerily over the highest. Mr. Bell said it was a cougar, and told her to be careful and perhaps take someone who could shoot when she went into the forest. Felicity scowled, and next day asked Chief Sealth about cougars.

"They are cats," he said. "Like your little friends. They look much like the lit-tle Shadow: tawny with a white muzzle, but very much larger and therefore not afraid—and so more friendly at heart. Sometimes they come to hunters' camps to get warm by the fire. More than once, a cougar has saved a wanderer from freez-ing on a cold night by curling up with him for warmth until morning. Cats kill to eat, but do not readily attack humans."

"Mr. Bell said—"

"White men are too quick to kill because they are aggressive, so they suppose all to be. But more often it is they who threaten. Someone who feels threatened, attacks, be it animal or human. What would Marilla do if you seemed to threaten her kittens or herself?"

"Oh!" said Felicity, but she frowned. "Well, but everyone says cougars chase people and attack them. They can't all be wrong, can they?"

The deep-set black eyes twinkled under jutting brows.

"Ah. Chase. Yes. A cat must always chase something that runs from it: this is the way the Earth Spirits made it. Dogs and men are not so very different, though they more often hunt in packs. But if you ever see a cougar, do not run away. Yell and wave your arms. Back away slowly. Or be small and still. Do not stare hard into its eyes. Rather, slowly close your eyes, or yawn, for a hard stare is a chal-lenge."

"I thought so!" crowed Felicity, and forgot about cougars, for her little cats were here and now, and only the next day Marilla came right up and sat studying her. Holding her breath, careful not to stare, Felicity stretched out a hand. Marilla sniffed it, found no food, and batted it away indignantly. Felicity jerked back in alarm—but then it occurred to her that the paw hadn't been loaded. The gesture was—what? A warning not to get cheeky? Felicity blinked slowly and tried again, Marilla batted again, still clawless, and this time Felicity left her hand where it was. Marilla sniffed it again, made a rude remark, and stalked back to her bush.

Never mind, it was great progress, and Felicity began, she thought, to under-stand their feelings—a bit. What she could not figure out was whether to call Shadow he or she.

In mid-February, she awoke earlier than usual on a cloudy morning that looked like all the others. But it felt different. There was something in the air that filled everyone with the most ridiculous high spirits. Olive and Virginia whirled out of bed and outdoors in their nightgowns, shouting and turning somersaults. A rabbit, doing very much the same thing out in the clearing, went right on doing it. The cats came out of their bush and had wrestling matches, the birds went wild, and Mr. Bell just chuckled when Vinnie splattered her porridge all over his full beard.

Laura nodded wisely, two dimples appearing in her ruddy cheeks. "It's the chinook," she announced. "Satco said it would come this week."

"I thought Chinook was the trade jargon," protested Felicity, who was feeling oddly like bursting into song even though she had not sung since leaving Virginia (and not much even there because Adelaide's soprano voice was so full that not even Mama ever noticed that Felicity's was low, sweet and true.)

"It's a magical kind of warm wind," said Mrs. Bell, and Felicity wondered doubtfully whether it was a tease. Skepticism crawled across her face and sat on her eyebrows; but the others just smiled mysteriously and told her to wait and see.

At noon the clouds suddenly melted away, leaving a dazzling sky of breath-taking blue. Against it, just visible between trees, Mount Rainier appeared, still looking unbelievable. Felicity had forgotten how high and white and majestic it was. The world was drowned in golden sunlight, and birds sang ecstatically, and chipmunks frolicked. The cats, tails and ears high, chased everything in sight including one another and a branch Mrs. Bell twitched for them. New leaves and shoots simply sprang into being, and a veil of pale filmy green began to appear as if by magic. The children took off shoes and stockings to frolic barefoot through the forest and down to the silver sand and over sun-warmed gray-weathered logs piled and tossed above the high-tide mark—and this time Felicity got up and down the bluff with very liitle trouble. The Indians left their winter lodges and came swarming back, camping on the smoothest bits of beach, from where they wandered about visiting their Boston tillicums (American friends), wandering in at any hour without so much as a knock.

Princess Kickisomlo, daughter of Chief Sealth, arrived one day thus unannounced. "I have new name now," she informed Mrs. Bell. "The new klootchman of Doc Maynard gave it to me. She said my name not pretty enough, and she will call me Princess Angelina."

Mrs. Bell lowered her head for a moment, suddenly much engrossed in the stocking she was mending. Felicity gazed in wonder at this Indian Princess—stocky, middle-aged, unlovely—who yet had an air of quiet royalty.

"That's a lovely name, and easier for us to remember," said Mrs. Bell after an instant. "It was friendly of Mrs. Maynard to think of it."

Angelina nodded gravely. "It is good. We are klosh tillicums. We help you live and find food. Now maybe some time you protect us if the Haidah or Tsimshian come down from the north in their big war canoes to mamook memaloose (make dead) and take slaves."

"Of course we will," agreed Mrs. Bell, and later she explained to Felicity that the warlike Indians from around Vancouver Island had a most unfriendly habit of swooping down in raiding parties—especially during chinook—and attacking the peaceful Puget Sound Indians.

"Our Indians believe fighting is an offense to the Earth Spirits, and silly, as well," she said wonderingly. "They don't think *things* are worth lives, so they just take to the woods until the raiders are gone. And they don't seem to care very much if their belongings are stolen or destroyed. Doc told me that Chief Sealth says 'people-things' don't matter, so long as no one can take away the 'spirit-things' like land and forest, water and sunshine." She sighed. "They don't even believe that land can be owned, for it belongs to the gods and spirits. What will they do, I wonder, when their Boston tillicums whom they trust, begin driving them from land and water. Then will they fight?"

"But we wouldn't!" bleated Felicity, shocked.

"Wouldn't we?" Mrs. Bell laid down the mended stocking and met Felicity's eyes challengingly. "We've done it everywhere we've settled, clear across the continent. So far, Seattle is less than a dozen households, most of whom hold the unusual idea that Indians are human beings. But more will come, and most of them will think of them as nothing but dirty Siwashes—Did you know that Siwash isn't a tribe; it comes from the word 'savage'?—who aren't even human."

"But they are!" Felicity bristled. "And they have a better right than we have; they were here first!"

"Oh, I agree," replied Mrs. Bell calmly. "But most folks don't. And you'll find that a lot of us white folk have funny ideas about our own superiority. For example—" and she looked at Felicity keenly. "—some people think it's all right to steal Africans from their homes and sell them into slavery."

"But—" Felicity stopped. Her eyes rounded. Mrs. Bell left her alone to cope with a shattering new viewpoint. The subject wasn't mentioned again.

There was little time to worry about past or future wrongs. Everyone was twice as busy while the chinook lasted—which was usually only a week or two, said Angelina. Making the most of it, other settlers helped Uncle Jon and Arne out on their claim beside Tenas Chuck, and at last the cabin was really going up—they said. Felicity, to her annoyance, had not yet been out to see the claim. But at least Uncle Jon dropped by every few days to tell her how the cabin was coming along.

Arne was visibly swollen with pride the day he killed a huge timber wolf right in their clearing. "He'll make a fine rug!" he bragged. "Maybe after we've moved in, Flissy can shoot us the rest of the family." The teasing missed its mark. Felicity had by now become thoroughly corrupted by Chief Sealth and her own instincts, and was not impressed.

"Did it actually attack you, or did you go out of your way to kill the poor thing?"

Arne's jaw dropped. Jon didn't really hear, being preoccupied with a new worry. "Honey, I don't want to put you in danger," he began uneasily. "Maybe—"

"Well, it's about a year too late to think of that!" Felicity snapped, one eye on the sudden hopeful gleam in Arne's. She tossed her head. "Still, if y'all are so worried, I reckon I'd better learn to shoot, hadn't I?" she remarked in a carefully off-hand voice.

Arne, she noted with satisfaction, looked distinctly baffled. She smiled, pleased. He instantly got back at her from another direction.

"Too bad you won't have a view in the new cabin."

Felicity promptly erupted. "What do you mean? You promised! You said we'd have a lovely view of the lake and mountains! Uncle Jon—" One eyebrow scrambled madly, and her lower lip was not only out, but quivering. Arne relented.

"Oh well," he amended with an annoying smile, "I suppose you might get a bit of view now and then when it isn't raining and you get brave enough to stick your head out the door. You weren't expecting glass windows, were you?"

His mouth curled widely as she suppressed an indignant sniff. She was improving, he decided with what he considered great tolerance. Not as whiny as she had been. And the short hair clustered loosely over her head really didn't look half bad. He wouldn't have said so for worlds. Nor would he have admitted how carefully he and Uncle Jon had planned the east wall to hold a window overlooking the lake and Cascade Mountains beyond.

It was going to be an unusual cabin when finished. "Part log, part split cedar like the Indians use," said Uncle Jon. "A one-room log cabin for now, rather like Bell's first one, so that we can move in as soon as possible. In two or three months the lumber mill will be running, and we can add another room of real boards for when your aunt and cousins arrive."

Felicity pushed that future time comfortably out of her mind. It was a long way off, and anyway, it was so hard to picture the exquisite Adelaide in a cabin in the wilderness, that the whole thing seemed quite unlikely. Instead, she went to the larder for some meat for the cats, who now came to meet her: Marilla and

Daffodil with raised tails, Shadow with a hiss and Tapestry with a whole diatribe on Dying of Hunger. Today, she vowed, Daffodil would eat from her hand.

Daffodil did his best. But never before having eaten from a hand, and unsure of what was being offered, the little creature manfully tried to chew Felicity's finger pads.

CHAPTER 9

▼

MANSION WITHOUT
WHITE PILLARS

Spring arrived, and with it came the Dexter Hortons, the Mercers, and Seattle's first wagon and team of horses. The town promptly appointed Tom Mercer its official teamster; and now that the lumber mill was finished, all the men pitched in to build the first road—out to the Mercer clearing.

The settled families cheerfully shifted around to take in the newcomers, though the Bells could not manage even one more. Now it was the Mercers who overflowed the old Bell house; and one day Laura, Satco and Felicity went over to visit. Laura and Satco took to Eliza right away, while Felicity and Mary Jane smiled at each other comfortably. The delayed friendship seemed, somehow, to have been quietly developing all by itself. "And I think we've both got more grown up, too," said Mary Jane wisely.

The chinook had broken, of course, into more rain. Much of it was that not-quite-wet variety (though Arne, back from a full day of working in it, denied this passionately.) But then came a truly violent storm, with winds funnelling northward between the two mountain ranges and lashing itself and everything else into a frenzy. Jon and Arne took refuge with the Bells on their way back from work on the new house, and stayed for supper, hoping for a break in the storm. But the rain still beat angrily upon the cabin roof, so that they all kept glancing up at it in awe. And then, in a brief moment of relative quiet, there came an imperious yowl from the door, along with angry scratching. They all stared, nonplussed. It came again, and this time there was no mistake: Felicity knew that voice.

"It's Marilla!" she cried, and flew to open the door before anyone could stop her.

In stalked a furious calico cat, fur so plastered to her skin that she looked like a wet otter, followed furtively by her sodden offspring. Marilla gave Felicity an accusing stare (clearly holding her responsible for weather as well as provisions), ignored everyone else, and marched over to the fireplace. There she siezed Shadow, her pet, by the scruff and proceeded to wash him thoroughly. Not to be intimidated, he began to groom her, as well, every time he could get his little white snout near enough.

Daffodil stared at the fire in total astonishment, clearly not sure whether it was predator or prey, until, perceiving the warmth, he lay down and stretched out blissfully. Tapestry lurked behind, ears flattened at all the strange giants, making a sharp spitting sound from the back of her throat, until she perceived a familiar shape and voice. Her ears rotated. She considered the matter, yawning as felines often do when uncertain. Then she made an astonishing choice. Ears folded fearfully down on her soaked skull, drenched body flattened to the floor, bragging in a series of tiny yelps and growls about How Brave she was Being, she crept slowly toward Felicity.

Felicity froze where she stood, incredulous. Tapestry reached her foot, sniffed it, spat, reached up to stick needle claws in her skirt, and began to tug. "Kneel very slowly," suggested Uncle Jon, holding his nearly emptied bowl of clam chowder ready to hand her.

Felicity obeyed, breathless. Tapestry reached her lap, hissed at the unexpected change, and then discovered that this new place was soft and warm and there was food hovering. She sniffed, found it acceptable, and finished it off. Then she permitted Felicity to rub the soaked fur with her woolen skirt, swore ungratefully, curled up in the lap, announced that it was Time to Sleep, and began a hoarse throbbing sound that vibrated through her beautiful small body.

"She's purring," breathed Felicity. "That's what it is, isn't it? I never had a cat in my lap before! I never heard one purr."

"Well, this one has you wrapped around her paw," oberved Uncle Jon with wry amusement. Felicity sat with the pulsating little creature in her lap, almost afraid to move. Her Tapestry! Hers! And just let anyone dare part them! If Arne could have Barf—

Dafodil, stretching ecstatically in the warmth, joined in with an even louder purr, suddenly broken off. He lifted his golden head, sniffed, and announced with a loud 'Prr-yow' that he smelled food. Marilla abandoned Shadow's bath, and they both demanded a share, as well. Mrs Bell obliged and for a few minutes the air was filled with ecstatic slurpings.

When they were done, Daff gave a last hopeful lick and returned to the hearth, but Shadow turned and judiciously surveyed his new surroundings. The champagne tips on each tawny hair looked almost irridescent in the firelight. Having considered matters, he marched purposefully up to each pair of feet in turn, lowering his white muzzle to sniff them solemnly, and then moving on. His tail was so erect it was forward over his back, causing Uncle Jon to peer hard and then grin.

"Well, at least now we know he's a boy." The grown-ups and Arne chuckled. Clearly they all knew something Felicity didn't, but she was not about to ask in front of everyone.

Shadow briefly licked Mrs Bell's foot, ignored Uncle Jon, and flattened his ears at Arne, who, he said indignantly, smelled of dog. At Mr. Bell he emitted a hoarse cry, like something between frog and cricket, rubbed a jaw on his boot— but then firmly removed himself to the delighted Laura. After that, Marilla agreed to settle on Mrs. Bell, and Daffodil—to whom it really didn't matter so long as it was warm, soft and dry, allowed himself to be picked up bonelessly and draped across Olive's lap like something freshly dead, head hanging over one side and tail the other.

The evening passed in something almost like reverence.

The storm ended soon after that, and Arne and Jon went home, but the cats firmly stayed inside, because, said Tapestry loudly, it was All Soggy Out There.

After that night, having Chosen, they came inside freely whenever it suited them. Marilla sniffed all over the cabin, approved, and took possession. Tapestry adopted Felicity as her Private Property, accepted Mrs. Bell, but threatened everyone else. Daffodil lolled near the cabin sleeping trustfully in any patch of sunlight, even when humans were around, (nearly getting himself stepped on half a dozen times a day) while Shadow behaved like the cougar he resembled, lurking and pouncing, 'killing' whatever stick or ball or foot or beetle came between his paws—though as Chief Sealth remarked with amusement, no cougar who ever lived had a voice like that.

And the sunshine came and went, and the forest bloomed, and Felicity spent hours walking and delighting in it. It spoke to her as the sea did to Arne; and she spoke back, imitating birds, telling a fragile, waxy-petalled trillium how lovely it was.

One day, in a marshy spot, she, Laura, Mary Jane and Eliza found what looked like masses of huge golden calla lilies.

"Spring candles is one name for them," Laura said gravely, and the others, rapturously picking, never noticed the impish glee in her hazel eyes.

"Skunk cabbages!" shrilled Olive when the girls appeared with their bouquet. "Oh, look, Ma! They brought skunk cabbages home just the way Laura did last year! They stink," she informed her abashed visitors importantly. "As soon as they get in the house, they stink almost as bad as skunks."

Laura grinned fiendishly. Felicity considered sulking. Then she looked at Mary Jane and Eliza, and a wonderful idea came to her. "Reckon you'll be seeing Arne tonight?" she suggested delicately. Mary Jane, who was wholly on Felicity's side in the running feud, dimpled. That evening the unsuspecting Arne was totally taken-aback to be offered an armful of golden lilies! And by a girl, too! Still, he'd always quite liked Mary Jane, so, much gratified, he took them ...

It set back his opinion of girls quite a lot.

Skunk cabbage and trilium were giving way to wild iris and violets when the Dare cabin was finally finished, and it was time to move in. "The cats, too," Felicity urged with the expression of a mother who might not be allowed to keep her children.

"All four?" Jonathan looked dismayed. Mrs. Bell came to his rescue.

"Could you leave Marilla and one of the boys with us?" she suggested. "We really need a mouser, and I think she's decided to live here, you know."

This was patently true: one look at her sitting possessively in the doorway proved it. "But won't she be lonely for her children?" Olive asked doubtfully.

"Not as children: they're nearly grown up now; but we should keep two each, so they'll all have company, and also produce new kittens. Everyone in town wants one."

Felicity sighed and agreed. She fussed over Marilla and brooded over which beloved boy to leave behind. But there was no decision, really. Shadow was clearly his mother's boy. So the other two (Tapestry yelling to be Rescued from Monsters, and trying to kill every hand that got near her, and Daff blinking affably and asking in his prr-ow chirp if it was dinnertime yet) were put into the crate that Mr. Bell had made. Barf (huge now and still growing) bounded around it like an amiable animated mountain. Tapestry told him at great length what she'd do if she ever Got Hold of Him. Daff just slitted his eyes and began to wash his sister. Barf, under the impression that all the world loved him, was impervious to their disapproval.

Uncle Jon shooed him away and checked the fastening.

"Don't let them get at Barf until they've accepted him," he warned the young'uns. (Arne snorted derisively.) "We'll just leave them in the cage until they feel at home in our new place. You don't want them coming back here."

Felicity privately didn't think they would leave her for anything, even the Bells. But what with one thing and another, she was so flushed with excitement by the time they were loaded and ready that Uncle Jon asked anxiously if she were fixing to be ill again, and then wondered why she snapped at him so fiercely.

All the same, when they had walked over from the Bell cabin to the new road, he insisted that she wait there for the wagon, and ride with the luggage as far as the Mercers' half-finished house—which was as far as the road went. Felicity didn't mind. Laura came with her, and the three older Mercer girls arrived in the wagon, and they laughed and chattered the whole way. But once they reached the Mercers' clearing, Felicity ran ahead the last half mile, leaving the other girls and the laden men behind. She wanted to see her new home first alone.

To the right, the clearing sprawled slantwise down the hill, hip-high with ferns and bracken, wild flowers and underbrush, nettles and blackberries, to the edge of the lake. New raw stumps were already vanishing beneath brambles and vines, but a number of trees had been left standing. Near the front door of the cabin, a black-trunked dogwood prepared to bloom, and there were Douglas fir, cedar, and a tall madrona tree, the thin red outer bark curling here and there to show the smooth pale green inner bark beneath.

Felicity gave it all one approving glance, and then sprinted along the path to the house. *Her* house. She paused in the doorway to stare in, eager-eyed. Everything was so deliciously, resin-scentedly new! It seemed fitting that she should be wearing newly cropped hair and the short-sleeved green and white gingham dress which Mrs. Bell had made her as a parting gift.

What a nice house it was, to be sure! Felicity permitted herself two tears of sheer joy as she stared around. Above, cedar slabs across the join of walls and roof made a very useful loft for insulation and for storing things. On this front wall, toward the lake, there was a window all ready to receive glass some day. On her left was another door, which would lead to the other room when it got built. The back wall, opposite, held a beautiful fireplace built of smooth sea-rounded stones and blue clay. It was, she noted approvingly, large enough to hold good-sized logs, and high enough for a spit and a swinging hook for the big iron kettle; and the dutch oven could go right there. And between fireplace and corner a large cupboard, not of split-cedar slabs, but real boards from the new lumber mill. She instantly decided to put the little stove between fireplace and cupboard, and the table right here, and this would be her kitchen. Her very own! She could hardly wait to start cooking all by herself!

The south-west corner seemed to be the bedroom. Cedar poles rose to the roof, complete with cedar slats with strong ropes woven across, to hold two mattresses, one above the other. Uncle Jon and Arne below, and she could have the upper all to herself. Lovely! Had a fairy godmother appeared then and offered to change the log cabin into a colonial mansion with white pillars and an army of smiling slaves, Felicity would have sent the fairy godmother packing.

"Move, idiot!" came Arne's voice from behind.

Felicity skipped hastily out of the way as he staggered in with a barrel of flour and headed for the nearest empty space, ably helped by a cavorting Barf. "Not there, stupid!" she ordered, getting her own back. "In that corner beside the cupboard. That's the kitchen, and besides, the other corner's going to have a hanging cupboard and dressing room. And you get out of here, Barf, this minute!"

Barf slunk out. Arne raised his bushy left eyebrow and lowered the flour. "Who says?" he challenged.

"I do!" she retorted. "This is where I do the bossing, Arne Knudsen! I'm the housekeeper, so I say what goes where, and if you don't mind me, I shan't fix you any dinner, so there."

This time Arne raised both eyebrows and his jaw sagged slightly. Flit? Housekeeping and cooking? Missy-Flissy? "I knew the excitement would be too much for you," he said kindly. "You'd better lie down and put some skunk-cabbage leaves on your head."

Felicity stamped a foot. "Over there!" she shouted, pointing an imperious finger at the chosen spot. Qualchan, entering just then with a keg of molasses and another of salt, took one look at this tenas klootchman on the warpath, and obeyed. And Arne, scratching his rumpled blond thatch, did likewise.

"I guess we'd better humour the lady," he observed with a shrug. "But, say, Fleecy, please don't try to cook for us! We're too young to die. Punish us any other way, but not that!"

Felicity turned her back. "All right, you can go hungry. The table goes here," she told Uncle Jon and Mr. Mercer as they brought it in. "And the bench beside it. Out, Barf! We'll have to use one stool to hold the wash basin until I can lash a stand for it; Satco showed me how. Soap and candles can go over by those barrels, and the trunks next the wall by the bed. Where are the quilts and mattresses and featherbeds? Uncle Jon, would you help Arne put them on the beds, please?"

"And what about this?" asked Mr. Mercer. 'This' was the crate of outraged cats. Barf at once rushed up to it again, tail rotating, barking horrendous greetings, pawing and sniffing. The crate spat at him. Felicity rushed over to croon endearments—but not to Barf.

"It's all right; nobody's going to hurt you; this is your new home; you mustn't be afraid of the nasty dog, darlings." The darlings, sounding far from frightened, swore and complained respectively. "You just stay away from them, Barf, if you know what's good for you," she threatened.

Barf, who clearly didn't, stuck a large wet nose between two of the the slats, yelped, and rushed outside. Arne followed, shouting indignantly.

"I warned him, and so did Uncle Jon," Felicity shouted after him, sorry about Barf, but definitely triumphant about Arne.

"Well, it's nice to see you feeling so perky, Felicity," Mr. Mercer said with a grin. "Mary Jane and Eliza and Susan are just behind, and I reckon you can borrow them as much as you want, to give you a hand." Felicity, who fully intended to do it all herself, smiled politely. Mary Jane would understand.

"Oh, I'd be so grateful," breathed Jon, looking at his niece worriedly. "You really mustn't try to do too much, honey. There's no Mrs. Bell to look out for you, and no point being foolish. Why not just sit down for a spell and order the rest of us around?"

Arne, returned from comforting Barf, snorted. So did Felicity. But then she discovered that she was a little tired, after all, so she ordered the yowling crate to be put in the quietest corner with plenty of food and water and the quilt over it, as Uncle Jon suggested. "Let them feel that they have a nice safe cave." Having done that, she seated herself with great dignity on one of the trunks and directed the unpacking from there, gloating privately over her new domain, enjoying the envy of the other girls.

Her very own little house! Tomorrow all the helpful neighbors would be gone and she would begin doing things herself. Cooking. Everyone had sent all kinds of food cooked and ready for tonight, but tomorrow was a new world, and there was so much to do!

She smiled.

CHAPTER 10

▼

"LITTLE WOMAN GO BANG!"

Arne looked with amazement at the large bowl of steamed clams and the crusty new-baked loaf of bread on the table, and then at Flit, busily digging baked potatoes from the ashes in the fireplace. "Mary Jane was over to fix supper?" he guessed.

If the potatoes hadn't been too hot to touch, Felicity would have thrown one at him. "Arne Knudsen, you're a mean ungrateful skunk!" she spat. "I cooked every bit of dinner myself, and you just needn't have any, so there!" She slapped the potatoes down on the table and seated herself with offended dignity.

Arne regarded her and supper from under a bushed eyebrow, and cautiously sampled a clam. "Holy Moses!" he discovered. "It's good!" He reached for another. Felicity, unmollified by this great praise, slapped his hand away.

"You can just mind your manners if you're fixing to eat my cooking! Wash your hands, and wait for Uncle Jon, and sit down properly, and we'll just say grace, too."

Arne opened his mouth angrily. But Jonathan, entering in time to hear it, spiked his guns. "She's quite right, Arne," he said, and led the way back out to the wash-up bowl.

Falicity flushed at being supported for once, and again when her uncle had tasted the still-warm bread. "Why, F'licity! I do believe you've a real gift for cooking! Reckon you got it from your grandmother." Pink with pleasure, Felicity at once began planning even better meals for him. But Arne, she decided, looking at him finishing off the clams and having another huge slice of bread, had got to be taken down a spell.

"I worked mighty hard on supper," she pointed out to Uncle Jon. "Arne's always bragging how big and strong he is, so I reckon he can just do the dishes."

"That's woman's work!" bleated Arne. Then he took a look at Flit's stormy brown eyes and suddenly realized that she had somehow got the upper hand. If he wanted to eat well in future—

"We'll do it together," Uncle Jon offered, which wasn't quite what Felicity had had in mind. "After all, we mustn't work our little girl too hard."

Stung, Felicity insisted on doing her share. "We've all worked all day, so we can share the washing up," she decided trenchantly. "And now," she announced when they were finished. "I'll let those poor little cats out of prison. Is everything shut tight so they can't get outside?"

"I was about to let Barf in," Arne gritted, determined not to give away any more points.

But once more Jon overrode him. "Be fair, Arne. It's still daylight, and he's fed, and has the whole outdoors to run around in; and the cats have been cooped up all day. They're part of the family too, you know. I think we can just let them loose to explore, honey."

The cats were not happy. Tapestry sat bolt upright, dark velvet ears rotated in annoyance, shouting in her piercing soprano that she had been Unjustly Imprisoned, and Where was Dinner? Even Daff lost his calm and chirped agreement.

When the cage was opened they hesitated, flattened their ears, crept out warily, and slunk around the edge of the room, bellies to floor and flanks pressed to the wall, commenting disparagingly. Too new, said Tapestry. The Wrong Smells. Not home, and where was Mum? added Daffodil. Passing the hearth where Felicity had set out a tasty meal for them, they paused, sniffed, and finished their tour. Then they continued around until they found supper again, looked at the humans severely, and crouched down to eat. That finished, they joined the humans in front of the fire. Only for a while, said Tapestry, and then she was Going Home. But presently Daff jumped to Felicity's chair, studied her lap for a moment, and flopped himself across it like a gold and white rug. Tapestry stared for a moment, whiskers angled back in annoyance, and then came and crashed herself down on top of him. Her Lap, she said.

"Oof!" said Felicity, delighted. But they were getting to be almost cat-sized by now, and her lap was insufficient, so presently Daff squirreled himself out from under and moved to Uncle Jon, who, he said, needed grooming. Arne stuck out his jaw and went to admit Barf, who wagged his tail mightily and settled down by the fire—at a safe distance from dangerous claws. And so the six of them enjoyed the peace and warmth of their brand new home.

But Felicity's mind was busy. She felt altogether proud and gratified, and on several counts. She had won two battles with Arne, Uncle Jon had backed her up (even though he had down-talked her stamina) the cats had chosen her lap—at least to start—and she had created a good meal. It was the first time in her life that she had really done something all by herself that was clever and useful. She was no longer a useless burden! She was a good cook, and about to become a better one.

It was unfortunate that her very next loaf of bread came out as hard and flat as a cedar slab, and on the very same day she burned the fish so badly that not even the cats would eat it. Tapestry, in fact, tried to bury it under the packed dirt floor. Nor did it help to have Uncle Jon tell her that it happened to all good cooks, even her grandmother. She felt utterly humiliated in front of Arne, who said he'd known she would try to poison him, and threatened to go eat with the Mercers. As the Mercers were still living in town at the old Bell place until their house was finished, Felicity just smiled nastily and said to go ahead because she wasn't cooking for him any more, and she hoped he starved on the way.

Arne observed that for a Delicate Constitution she had a mighty poisonous tongue; and at that point it occurred to Jon that they were rather overdoing the playful banter. He said so, and the quarrel ended in astonished silence. Playful banter?

After a few days, the cats decided to accept their new home, and were left out of the crate for good. Barf was again introduced to them, and whined cautiously. Tapestry batted at him again—but with sheathed claws—told him to Watch It, and then went to see if he'd left any breakfast. Daff (who loved grooming almost as much as sleeping) began assiduously to wash the dog's startled face. Barf, panting affably, permitted it. In that moment the cats became secondary pack-leaders. (They did not know this, of course. Pack-leader—or even pack—was a concept totally incomprehensible to the feline mind. As far as Tapestry and Daffodil were concerned, they had Their Human, and were willing to live in harmony with a few assorted other life forms—conditional, of course, on their good behavior.)

The days raced by. There was so much to do! The Mercers' cabin was finished in record time, and they moved in; and the girls visited back and forth almost daily. But much as she enjoyed the novel delight of having friends, Felicity was still wrapped up in the joys of her new house. Soon there were Indian mats beside the wolfskin on the floor, a gift from Princess Angelina; and a Felicity-lashed wash-stand just outside the door that was only the tiniest bit wobbly, and when she found time she'd do a better one. The beds were bright with gay quilts; and Uncle Jon put pegs in the wall and a rod across the back corner on which Felicity hung a hand-woven counterpane for a curtain—and lo, she had her dressing room and hanging cupboard.

Mama's two silver candlesticks and teapot (the only true luxuries to survive the journey) stood on the table; and there was the big lamp with a mantle for reading by (when the books should arrive) and two little tin lamps with a braided rag wicks in which they burned dogfish oil. This made a dim and smelly light and was always leaking; but Felicity had not yet learned to make candles, and they were costly to buy; and dogfish oil could always be traded from the Indians. Bit showed her a dead dogfish once; it looked like an eighteen-inch shark.

Both Arne and Uncle Jon began working part-time at the mill, but at least one of them was always around the cabin with Barf, working on the new wing or digging up more garden beds. Although Mr. Mercer left his girls most days while he hauled logs with his wagon and team, Uncle Jon did not feel easy about poor fragile Felicity being alone. It was true that the Indians were friendly to all and particularly fond of the Dares and Mercers. It was also true that Felicity had been practicing with the rifle ever since early March, and even Arne admitted that she was getting to be a good markswoman. But Jon still thought of her as a frail and timid little thing—and after all, this was wilderness. Cougars prowled. Unpredictable brown bears and nasty-tempered black ones roamed the forest with their playful and inquisitive cubs—and even a brown bear with cubs is no one to fool around with!

A sound of cats yowling and hissing brought Arne in from work on the new wing one sunny afternoon to see Felicity staring with startled delight at a small bundle of brown fur that had coolly walked in. Barf was nowhere to be seen, the two cats were swearing luridly from atop the sagging dressing room curtain, and the cub had a purposeful eye on a platter of fish.

"Oh, no, you cunning naughty thing!" Felicity scolded, snatching it away.

Arne wasted no time on admiration. A glance through the open door showed him exactly what he feared: the shaggy bulk of mama bearing down like a brown-furred avenging Fury to protect her child.

In one swift motion Arne scooped up the bewildered cub, thrust it outside, and slammed the door in mama's infuriated face. Then he leaned against it for a moment, listening to her dire threats fade into the distance.

"Whew!" he observed, and looked sternly at Felicity. "I hope you got the lesson."

Felicity noted with wonder that the freckles stood out blotchily against his suddenly pale face, and nodded meekly. "I—I reckon I didn't know bears had such tempers," she murmured in awe.

"Well, now you know!" scolded Arne. "No more playing with cubs! And see to it your rifle's in reach all the time; and you're never to go anywhere without it. Understand? Holy Moses, Flit, why do you think Uncle Jon went to so much trouble getting you the smallest and best one he could find?"

Felicity's temporary meekness evaporated. "I know!" she snapped. "And I do all that, and I wasn't playing with him, he just dropped in to visit, and you don't expect me to shoot a sweet innocent baby bear that didn't mean anything wrong, do you?"

Arne recovered his derisive grin. "Female logic! No, silly, but you might have stopped it from coming inside—"

Felicity remembered something. "I thought that was what Barf was supposed to do, and where is he, anyway?"

Where indeed? Dead at the long curved claws of mama bear? In sudden panic, they both began calling frantically, and were deeply annoyed when he showed up presently, huge and gormless, right across the vegetable garden, his tail rotating joyously, dripping with lake water. Felicity, pointing out that her cats were better watchdogs than his monster, took down her rifle and marched over to visit Mary Jane. Arne, shaking his head, went back to work until Qualchan came by, and the two of them got off into the fascinating business of canoe-building.

Qualchan and Arne were together whenever they could manage it, which was much of the time. The Mercer girls popped over almost daily, Satco and Bit visited often, and sometimes Laura came with them. Chief Sealth made a point of dropping by now and then, usually with Doc, to see Felicity, approve all she had done since the last visit, sample her cooking, and give her a lesson in Duwamish. It was clear that both men were pleased with her.

"Strong shining thoughts," observed the chief, looking with approval at her glowing face. "Very good."

But some of the other Indians were a mixed blessing. They had their own rules of hospitality. Total strangers were likely to walk in at any time, wanting to trade something or just pass the time of day. If they sat on the bed, they usually left dirty marks and fleas behind them—a gift which Jon and Arne, who slept in the lower bunk, found particularly annoying. And one day Felicity turned just in time to see a hulking young brave putting her freshly baked loaf of bread into his greasy shirt.

She promptly turned herself into a solecks (mad) tenas kootchman.

"Massachie cultus Siwash!" she stormed. "Give that back! Hyas! Quick! Now!"

Sheepishly the Indian obeyed. He wasn't really hungry; it had been just an impulse. And Flit was the Klosh tillicum of Chief Sealth, who would be much soleks if he found out about this.

"Tenas klootchman mamook pooh," he observed admiringly. "Hiyu skookum, much brave. Klahowyah," he added, leaving.

"Klahowyah," she responded thankfully as he walked away. Then she grinned. Mamook pooh, make bang, was the Chinook description for shooting a gun. Had she been that fierce? she asked Daffodil, who had just settled himself in the sunshine in the middle of the doorway.

He prrowed assent and looked hopefully at her hair, which he groomed, of late, every time he could get to it. Felicity chuckled, wiped off her rescued bread, stepped over the cat, and went out to work in her new garden.

She was out there again after supper, loving the long twilight that slowly bleached all the color from earth and sky, leaving everything in muted mauve and taupe and gray. The cats bounded past her, stopped a little way ahead at some shadowy bushes, and paused, clearly passing the time of day with something or other. She had seen them do that before. Now she moved closer, stepping delicately, thankful that the light had not yet gone as she peered toward those bushes.

From them, one by one, marched a parade of six small creatures, kitten-sized, little pointy noses cockily upward, bushy black and white striped tails aloft. They paused, looked at the cats. Glee seemed to hang in the air. Daffodil pounced. And instantly a full-fledged game of tag was in progress. Around and around they went, leaping and rolling, skittering around Felicity's ankles, occasionally pausing to raise their tails and point little butt ends at one another. The delighted Felicity was almost sure she know what the little creatures were and even what that butt-pointing was all about, but it was so patently all in fun that she wasn't the least bit worried.

And at one point the liveliest of the visitors rocketed up to her, crashed sideways against her ankle, paused, peered upward in what seemed to be long contemplation—and then, quite deliberately, sat down on her bare foot with its hot little bottom. She promptly named it Miss Muffet, and walked back to the cabin in full dusk with shining eyes and the air of a maiden in love.

"What were you doing just standing out there?" Arne demanded as if he had a right to know. She ignored him. And it wasn't until the next day that she oh-so-casually asked her question.

"Uncle Jon, are skunks and cats friends?"

"Shouldn't think so. Why?"

"Well, they're about the same size, Mary Jane says, so I wondered."

"Things the same size needn't be friends, silly!" Arne pointed out derisively. "Cat's'd be sorry, I expect. Qualchan says skunks spray almost as soon as they can walk. Look what happened to Barf!" he added feelingly, and they all shuddered. Barf had run into the cabin to escape the searing stench, and they had all had to camp outside for days.

"Why, honey; have you seen a skunk?" Uncle Jon asked solicitously. You want to stay right away from them, now, won't you?

"Mmm," said Felicity non-committally, and went out again that dusk to play cat-and-skunk tag and coax Miss Muffet to sit on her foot again.

On May 23, Felicity was awake at the crack of dawn. It was a holiday, when all Seattle would gather to file the plats. Felicity wasn't quite sure what plats were, but she thought it was a kind of map of the town with streets marked off and named. The proper town, so far, was only on the Boren, Denny and Maynard properties, plus Mr. Yesler's strip (named Mill Street but usually called Skid Road for the lumber skidding down it to the waterfront and the waiting ships). But it was a beginning, and when the plats were all properly filed in Mr. Yesler's cook-house, and then sent to Oregon City, then Seattle would be a real official town. Doc Maynard, whose property was south of Mill Street, said that the streets ought to follow the compass. But Mr. Denny and Mr. Boren said they should follow the shore line which bent to the northwest above Mill Street. Neither side would give in. A hundred years from now, Arne predicted ghoulishly and accurately, Seattle's streets would meet at Yesler's street at a weird angle and everyone would wonder why.

Felicity didn't really care. This was a holiday, and the birth-day of Seattle, and the first time she'd been back to town since they moved out here.

She climbed briskly down from her upper bunk, fed Barf and the cats, started breakfast, and dug down to the bottom of her clothes box for the one party dress she had brought from Virginia. It was much too fancy even to have considered wearing any time since leaving home—but this was a special occasion. She held it up: the dainty rose-sprigged dimity with tucks, embroidery, and lace on the short sleeves, and a pink silk sash.

But when she put it on, in the narrow space of her little curtained corner, something seemed to be wrong. She struggled with the buttons for a while— (Viola had always put it on her before)—and then called on Uncle Jon for help.

He laughed when he saw her. "My stars, F'licity, how you've grown! Here, hold your breath, honey, and I'll try to button you."

But it was quite impossible. The sprigged dimity was laid aside for Susan (who would squeal with delight over it) and Felicity put on the yellow muslin frock that Mary Jane had passed down to her. She'd never been able to wear yellow: it made her skin hideously sallow, so she peered doubtfully in the tiny mirror hung above the washstand just outside the door. But it looked all right now her face was tanned and her cheeks just faintly pink. And in the delicious May sunshine her hair (no longer limp) gleamed with warm red-gold highlights. She smiled.

"Look at Flit flirting with herself!" jeered Arne, sticking his head out the door. Felicity tweaked his ear, hard.

"Come along, you two," ordered Jon. "We should be over at the Mercers' in twenty minutes if we don't want to miss the wagon."

They went. But Felicity kept a baleful eye on Arne's back as they single-filed along the forest path. Why, she began to ask herself, should he do all the teasing?

From the Mercers' they all rode to town in style, with Barf bounding along-side, the two men up in front, the five girls laughing and chattering in the back of the wagon, and Arne stranded in between. Girls! he thought, keeping himself loftily aloof from the bevy of giggling females. He should have known better. For young Eliza possessed both a sharp eye and a wicked tongue. Presently she turned both upon Arne. "I guess he thinks he's too good to associate with us," she observed impudently.

Five pairs of critical young eyes fixed themselves upon him uncomfortably. Arne was always willing to match wits with one or even two girls at a time, given the superior advantage of maleness, but these odds were a bit unfair. He chose disdainful silence as his best weapon.

Felicity looked at him. A light began to dawn. Could one get back at Arne with his own weapons? She raised a mocking eyebrow. "Oh, Arne reckons he's just terribly grown-up and important," she drawled sweetly. "The way he tries to boss me around sometimes, you'd think he was my grandpa."

Arne countered this with two mocking eyebrows and a quelling grin. The girls failed to be quelled. "If he's as grown-up as all that," Eliza observed fiendishly, "he'd better hurry up and get married."

"Ugh!" said Arne with feeling.

They giggled at him. "How about Mary Jane?" chortled Susan. "She's just the right age." Mary Jane made a sick face and told Susan not to spoil her breakfast.

Arne reddened, knew it, reddened all the more. "Girls!" he observed disgustedly to a large fir beside the road. "Why were the silly things ever invented?"

But his comment was lost in shrieks of laughter, even from Mary Jane. They had scored and they knew it. Felicity in particular knew it. Her eyes, dancing with triumph, rested thoughtfully on the uncomfortable figure of her irritating foster-cousin. She smiled. Arne Knudsen might not know it yet, but a new era had just dawned.

CHAPTER 11

▼

THE INCOMPARABLE
ADALAIDE

Arne stood in the middle of the new room and looked around with satisfaction. Nearly finished. Only a few more touches, in fact. The weather had held! He could be through in an hour and still have time to be out in the glorious July sunshine before Uncle Jon got back from town.

For the summer had made up for the winter. Even now, long blue and golden days dreamed by, deliciously warm, but without the savage heat of Illinois or Virginia. Now and then some rain glittered the world, causing leaves and grasses to burst into new richness of green; and the little lake (which Doc Maynard predicted would one day be circled with homes) mirrored the fir-covered hills in shimmering wet crystal. Now that he and Qualchan had finished the canoe, Arne spent nearly every free moment out in it. He even took Felicity along now and then in an apricot and amber sunset or the long blue twilight of the late summer evenings.

Flit, it occurred to him vaguely, had much improved lately. No longer a whiny invalid, she—well, she wasn't bad—for a girl. True, she had got awfully sassy suddenly, since a certain day in May, but—Arne shrugged. He wouldn't admit even to himself that he quite enjoyed the challenging and amusing person she had become. It was, he decided, her cooking, which got tastier every day. It was as a reward for that, he assured himself, that he took her out, and had even taught her to paddle.

Tapestry, who had long ago decided to accept Arne, strolled up, rubbed sinuously and condescendingly around his ankles, and hissed, just in case he should get Above Himself. She reminded him strongly of Flit. They'd both grown a lot, both composed of quite lovely mixtures of brown-copper-bronze-gold, and both distinctly uppity. He grinned.

There was a patter of bare feet from the next room and Felicity appeared in the doorway, a basket of early wild blackberries and red huckleberries over one arm, her rifle in the other.

"Pie for supper if you're good," she announced.

There being nothing much better than one of Flit's pies, made with the tiny tart-sweet wild berries, Arne reluctantly decided against any justified comments about her appearance. Her newly-cropped curls were a wild bronze tangle, her tanned face was flushed and streaked with dirt. Seven golden freckles adorned her tilted nose. Hands and feet were scratched, brown and berry-stained. And last spring's green gingham dress was not only the worse for wear, but already getting too small.

Arne, suddenly remembering the scrawny weepy doll-baby he had first seen in Independence over a year and a half ago, dressed in a froth of pink ruffles, grinned broadly and cast his good resolutions to the winds. "Have a fight with a bear?" he inquired kindly.

"Might as well have," she retorted, failing to rise to his teasing. She pushed her hair back from a damp forehead, leaving another streak of dirt behind. "Fought with nettles, devil's club, oregon grapes, dewberries, thistles, brambles, salmonberries, salal, blackberries, huckleberries—"

"Huckleberries don't have thorns or stingers," interrupted Arne.

"I fought with them all the same," she maintained with dignity. "While you and Daff were probably napping," she added unfairly, looking at the nearly-grown gold and white cat sleeping in the exact centre of the new room in a totally unlikely positon, on his back, all four legs hanging limply in mid-air.

It really was a very nice room, fully as large as the first, and also with a door and fireplace and half-loft, so that it could become the main room and kitchen. The half-loft was made by running cedar slabs across where walls and roof joined. There was a ladder built up the wall to it, and it would be very useful some day when six people lived here instead of only three. Already the old room was cleverly divided by curtains into three separate bedrooms. A double bed in one, for Uncle Jon and Aunt Julia; double bunks in the other two: one for boys and one for girls. (Felicity, who loved her current upper bunk, had already laid claim to this one.) Each alcove had several wall pegs, and space for clothes chests. And the new room could become the main room almost at the drop of a hat: just by moving things in. The old Virginia mansion had become dim and remote in Felicity's memory.

"Have you fixed that loose board at the back of the loft yet?" she demanded.

Just like a girl, to overlook all he had done and pounce on the one thing he hadn't got round to yet!

"You go build your pie, Missy-Flissy," he advised her briskly. "I'll be done before you are. And if it's a good pie," he added insultingly from halfway up the ladder, "I might even take you canoeing tonight."

Felicity threw a berry at him, missed, and turned into the old room, humming contentedly and nearly tripping over Daffodil, who flicked an ear, stretched, and went on sleeping.

Life was wonderful these days, now that Arne was becoming civilized. Mutual teasing was fun, they had both learned. Canoeing, too. Not that there was a lot of time these days for canoeing or teasing—or walking in the woods, or playing with the cats and Barf, for that matter. There was cleaning and scrubbing and clothes-washing and ironing and cooking and growing vegetables. Potatoes and onions and beets and string beans—Still, she managed to fit in a flower garden, too. The bit of sweetbriar that Louisa Denny gave her, and things like foxglove, bleeding heart, harebells, and those wild sweet peas with their pinky-purple clusters …

Felicity frowned. Those sweet peas had done a little too well. They were threatening to take over the whole garden. She must do something to discourage them a little.

She finished rolling the pie crust, slid it carefully on to the pan, and thought about supper. The string beans were picked, and the trout ready to bake, and the potatoes could bake, too … Engrossed in pie and plans, she only half noticed a shape standing in the open doorway. Since it didn't call her by name, it was probably just a strange Indian dropping by, and she was too busy sugaring the berries and piling them in the pan to look up quite yet.

"Klahowyah," she murmured politely but absently.

No answer.

"Itka mika tickey?" (What do you want?) She carefully put the top crust on, trimmed and pinched the edges, and began to notice a kind of baffled silence behind her.

It was broken by an equally baffled voice. A familiar voice, but with an unfamiliar note of uncertainty. "I—I thought my cousin lived here?"

Felicity turned. There—lovelier than ever, golden curls brushed up into a cluster, with stylish lavender-blue dress and bonnet fresh and immaculate—stood Adelaide.

It wasn't fair! Felicity had almost made herself believe it would never happen—and now it had! Here she was, beautiful and clever and talented and ladylike: her unbearably superior cousin! Felicity just stood there, reduced to what she'd been back in Virginia: awkward, tongue-tied and altogether inferior. Tapestry put a head inside, paused with flattened ears, spat, and rushed past the strange human, to jump on the table and shout that No Strangers were Allowed.

Cousin Charles' long head appeared over Adelaide's. He frowned. "Is Miss Felicity Dare here? Are you the servant? Speak up, girl."

Felicity didn't really notice what he was saying, for part of her mind was crying that her happiness was over forever, and part of it was thinking that she'd never seen Charles look discombobulated before, and the rest of it was wondering wildly if there would be enough supper for all of them.

She whispered "Come in," and turned blindly away. She mustn't cry! Arne would lose all respect for her. Blinking, she slit the top crust and stooped to slide her pie into the dutch oven ... Oh dear, perhaps she'd better bake another one! If Aunt Julia—But Aunt Julia would be mistress of the house now, and not Felicity! She bit her lip but a tear came anyway.

"What's the matter?" asked Uncle Jon's cheerful voice from the doorway. "Well, this is it, Julia; come on in. Why, F'licity, honey, aren't you going to greet your aunt and cousins?"

There were two gasps and two stunned echoes. "F'licity?"

Felicity smeared off the tear—incidentally spreading little more dirt around her face—straightened, and turned to look at her cousins. Their faces were two blank blobs of disbelief. Aunt Julia took a good look, became a third blank blob, and sat down weakly on the nearest stool. Tapestry retreated under the table, from where she threatened to Have Their Guts for Garters. Uncle Jon suddenly laughed. "Why, didn't you-all recognize her?" he demanded, and then turned to study his niece. "Well, no," he conceded, "I reckon you wouldn't."

"Recognize her! I still don't!" Aunt Julia declared. "Great day in the morning, I can't believe it!" She didn't say whether or not she approved the change.

Adelaide clearly didn't. "Oh, F'licity!" she cried sympathetically. "Honey, what's happened to you? Your poor hair! And your complexion looks like a wild

Indian! You've got freckles! And bare feet! Why, you look like White Trash! Father, what sort of dreadful place is this?"

Felicity bristled. She completely forgot how superior Adelaide was. No one was going to insult her lovely home, her Promised Land! "It's a wonderful place!" she snapped. "And I cut my hair because I wanted to, and I like bare feet, too, so there!"

Adelaide gaped, quite dumbfounded. Why, F'licity had never in all her life sassed her back, before! But whatever she might have said in reproof was lost forever. It had finally dawned on Arne, under the eaves in the new room, that something out of the ordinary was going on. He appeared in the doorway, took one look at the angelic beauty of Adelaide, reeled under the impact of huge blue-violet eyes framed in silken fans—and fell hopelessly in love.

Jonathan, blissfully unaware of the various storms raging about him, beamed. A big happy family at last. "Arne! Come and meet your new aunt and cousins. He's one of the family now, Julia; we'd never have managed without him. Adelaide—Charles—Charles is just a year older than Arne, so you two can be great friends; and the girls will have a wonderful time together, too, won't you? What a lucky thing I went into town today! There was a schooner just arriving from San Francisco, and there they were! Mercer brought us most of the way in his wagon, and we'll go fetch the trunks later."

"How d'y'do," managed Arne, unable to take his eyes off the vision in blue.

Adelaide, with sure feminine instinct, smiled enchantingly and lowered demure lashes with devastating effect.

Felicity, who had some sound feminine instincts of her own, stared at Arne with a deep sense of betrayal. Arne the strong-minded, the independent, the girl-hater! And he had fallen without so much as a struggle! It was only to be expected, of course, Adelaide being Adelaide. All the same, Felicity felt outraged and disillusioned. She turned a contemptuous back on Arne (who never noticed) and eyed Aunt Julia, who, though clearly dismayed, at least was making gallant attempt to admire her new home.

Charles wasn't. "Land o' Goshen!" he bleated in the tones of one who has been confidently expecting white-pillared colonial mansions. "I thought—I didn't expect it to be quite so primitive, Father! Your letter made it sound like a proper town." He eyed Arne's wolfskin rug as if it might snap at him, and then looked around the room. "Where do the servants live?" he asked innocently.

Arne tore his fascinated gaze away from Adelaide long enough to look at Charles with disdain. "Right here," he said briefly. "Six of us. How are you at chopping wood?"

Felicity would have chortled had she not been so upset. Charles looked lofty and disbelieving, and changed the subject. "We brought all those books you insisted on, Father, and your violin, though I can't see what use they'll be in a—a wilderness like this." He turned a cool shoulder to Arne, clearly doubting that such White Trash could even read. "And where on earth can we put them? Or my riding habit and dress clothes, for that matter?"

"Oh, you won't need silly clothes like that," Felicity told him kindly. "And we'll just build book cases, and they can go right against this wall. We can get real boards from Mr. Yesler, but I could lash one of sticks until then; I'm quite good at it. I did the wash stand out front."

Charles blinked down his long nose at her. Adelaide looked pained. Jonathan under the impression that everyone was getting on splendidly, beamed. "What a joy to have books and music again! Now we can sing and read aloud in the evenings, and with more of us to help with the work, perhaps now Seattle can set up some sort of school. There must be twelve or fifteen young'uns here now. Charles could help teach."

Charles pretended not to hear. Adelaide raised pleading eyes to her sire. "Father, you can't really mean we're all to live in just two rooms!"

Felicity blinked and turned to Arne, who should by now have been jibing about fussy doll-babies. But Arne was clearly thinking that Adelaide deserved a palace at the very least. All to herself. Abandoned, Felicity challenged her cousin for the second time. "Why, there's heaps of room! Even more than the Bells have, and there were seven of us in there for a while. This is one of the biggest cabins in Seattle, Adelaide! We built that whole second room especially for when you folks came."

Adelaide gave her the pitying look that had always reduced Felicity to about two feet high, and it did so now. A withering glance from Arne crushed her still further.

"Reckon I'd better look at my pie and start supper," she mumbled, turning away. "Arne, you can just go pick some more beans and dig the potatoes and fetch the fish out of the spring, and you'd best bring the rabbit, too, y'hear?" She turned to the arrivals. "If y'all want to freshen up, the wash-stand is outside the door, and mind you don't let Barf help you. Aunt Julia, Uncle Jon will show you your bedroom, and Adelaide, your bed is the lower one in the far corner to the right."

"Why, honey!" exclaimed Aunt Julia, her soft rosy face puckering with surprise. "Have you been cooking and keeping house for these two strapping menfolk all by yourself? You clever child! Just wait till I freshen up a mite, and then you tell me what I can do to help." Felicity discovered that she had never properly appreciated Aunt Julia, who was giving Felicity the praise and admiration she longed for. And went on doing it, too. "Honey, I think it's just remarkable the way you've blossomed, and all you've been doing! I declare, you're a real pioneer, and you put me to shame. I hardly know how to boil water, so you're just going to have to teach me everything."

Felicity glowed.

So did Uncle Jon. "Adelaide, too," he pronounced blithely. "What more could a man want than three women to cook delicious meals, eh, Arne?"

Adelaide, seated uncomfortably on the one chair with a back, said nothing, but her sweet smile covered some very confusing emotions. Cooking! That was for slaves to do! For the first time in her life she felt out of place and—well—downright inadequate. And she had a feeling that riding to hounds, embroidery, and painting on china were not properly appreciated in this place. She didn't like the feeling. Arne's adoration was all very well, but he was just a country bumpkin: Yankee, at that. And there was F'licity …

The more Adelaide looked at F'licity, the more she disliked the way her sickly no-count cousin had changed. The dreadful cropped hair and tanned face, though unladylike, were becoming. She had grown taller, and become wiry rather than skinny; her face was no longer peaked, but—piquant—and her eyes! How was it she had never noticed how large and sparkling they were? Heaven's to Betsy! F'licity was getting downright pretty! Not that she could ever compare with Adelaide's own spun-gold beauty, but all the same—

She looked across the room at the brown capable hands swooping a pie out of the oven and back again, and almost in the same movement doing something efficient-looking with several snowy-white fish and a dismembered rabbit. The drooping mouth had become firm with new self-assurance, and had a suggestion of impish humor lurking at the corners. And, Adelaide remembered, F'licity had sassed her back, not once, but twice. And might well go on doing it, too, from the look of her.

But Adelaide was not one to pull down her flag easily. She'd already put F'licity in her place once that day, and could do it again. "Whatever was that quaint gibberish you were talking when I first came, F'licity?" she inquired in the crushingly tolerant voice one used when being kind to a slave.

This time her cousin failed to be crushed. She was busy with the trout. "Hmm?" she asked absently, reaching out to push the pot of beans back over the fire. "Oh—I remember. I thought you were an Indian, so I reckon I was speaking Chinook."

Aunt Julia stopped setting the table. Charles tore his eyes from the astonishing scenery outside the front door. Three shocked faces tried to digest the implications of this casual remark.

"You mean," asked Adelaide carefully, "that wild Indians actually walk right up to the door?"

The voice penetrated Felicity's abstraction. She lifted her head, and met those blue eyes squarely with her own brown velvet ones for the first time in her life. She blinked. A slow diabolical smile crept over her face—to be replaced at once by wide-eyed candor.

"Oh, they don't just come to the door, Addie. Not usually." She paused tantalizingly to measure flour for the biscuits and have a word with a much-annoyed tortoise-shell cat. "Arne, Tapestry's thirsty and my hands are floury; could you fill her water dish? Oh yes, the Indians." She flicked an artless glance at her once-patronizing cousins, now hanging on her every word. "Well, they usually just walk in without knocking, and sit down on the beds and leave fleas there; and once a great big brave tried to steal my fresh-baked bread ... There you are, sweet Tapestry," she added, stroking the indignant cat. "Reckon you'd best get used to all these people, honey." She turned back to the dutch oven with bland unconcern.

The speechless silence lasted quite a few seconds. Then Charles broke it.

"But F'licity—Well, what did you do, for mercy sake?"

"Well, I made him give it back, of course," said Felicity in genuine surprise. "What else?"

CHAPTER 12

▼

FELICITY'S WAR

Felicity dug in her garden so furiously that the weeds hadn't a chance, and even the beets looked faintly alarmed. She seemed quite capable of pulling them up, too. Tapestry, who had taken to following her around the garden with waving tail and voluble comments about Mice and Beetles and Gophers, watched approvingly. But Felicity scowled. She hated nearly everything (except the animals) these days. Most of all she hated having been returned implacably to her old role of Poor Felicity, the inferior cousin. No matter that the role no longer fit her any more than did the pink sprigged dimity; she seemed unable to strip it off and throw it away.

She pulled up a beet. She looked at it. "Oh, I'm sorry," she muttered, and put it back in the ground. Then, sitting back on her heels, she wiped her damp forehead with the back of her arm, scratched the base of the delighted Tapestry's ears, and looked around the peaceful sunny clearing, still a bit damp from last night's shower.

Aunt Julia was in the house sewing on a much-needed new dress for Felicity, perhaps, or gamely struggling with housework. Felicity now loved her more than any other human. For, unlike her children, Aunt Julia had totally dropped Virginian thinking and set about learning to be a pioneer wife. She was, her niece hoped, beginning to enjoy it as Felicity did.

Her cousins were a different matter. Adelaide seemed to think that if she sat around looking beautiful and helpless long enough, someone would come wait on her—and she was right. Arne inevitably did. And somehow it had never occurred to anyone, not even Felicity—yet—that the decorative Adelaide ought to be pulling her weight.

As for Charles, he had gone into a state of shock. Being even more useless at practical matters than his father had been, he came to grief at anything he tried. He mashed his thumb and also the chicken house he was trying to help build, and he cut his foot instead of the wood he was supposed to be chopping, and he always managed to slop half the water out of the buckets before he got to the house with them—even without the help of Barf, whose favorite new game was to put his forefeet on Charles' shoulders and see if he would fall down. (He frequently did.) And he and Arne each kept looking at the other as if they'd been cleaning the out-house—a point on which Felicity tended to agree with both of them.

Uncle Jon finally noticed this (with considerable help from Aunt Julia) and astonished his family with the firmness of his action. He packed Charles down to the lumber mill and told Mr. Yesler to find something he could do and pay him what he was worth. If anything.

Mr. Yesler saw at once that he needed Charles' brain rather than his brawn, and put him in the office. Charles discovered to his considerable astonishment that he had the makings of a good business man. He wrote brisk clear letters, organized accounts, and developed a deep interest in the lumber business. As a result, he no longer walked around trying to be a gentleman and feeling like a salmon on dry land, he stopped looking down his nose at everything, and he and Arne began to tolerate each other.

Which was fine for them, but didn't help Felicity. Her world had been thrown into another tangle, just as she'd sorted the first one out. Moreover, she missed her friends. Since Adelaide was persistently terrified of Indians, Satco and Bit—along with Laura—stopped visiting, and even Qualchan seldom came to the house any more. The Mercer girls resented Adelaide's airs, so they stopped coming, too. Really, there were only the cats and Miss Muffet and Aunt Julia now, for her dawning friendship with Arne had been completely wiped out. He had spent several days in a kind of coma, brought on by his sudden and violent attack of first love. And now … Felicity, seeing two fair heads down by the lake, scowled. Then she got to her feet, brushed off the bits of black earth, and wandered wistfully down the hill. Tapestry, stepping high over the tall grass, tail erect, followed.

Arne pulled the canoe near the bank, so that Adelaide could step in easily. He stamped on a thistle lest she should touch it. He ordered Barf to keep his distance. For Adelaide was a gentle creature, easily frightened by large dogs and Indians, clearly intended by nature to be beautiful and inspiring rather than useful. She needed to be cherished and protected—unlike Flit, who, he noted absently, was coming down the slope toward them followed by both cats. The disloyal Barf streaked joyously to meet her—and actually lowered his big head so that Daff could wash it more easily.

Arne felt vaguely displeased with all of them, for somehow trying to make him feel that Adelaide compared in any way whatever to what Flit had been. Flit, he remembered vividly, had been whiny, self-pitying and in need of discipline. Adelaide was beautiful, truly helpless, and very patient with this hard new life. And she rewarded any small service with a delightful smile and melting glance. She did so now. "It's so sweet of you to take me canoeing," she murmured. "Mind, I'd be right scared with anyone but you, Arne."

Arne glowed. "Wait until I take you out at sunset."

Felicity heard that last remark as she reached the lake, practically surrounded by Barf, who was trying with some success to wash both her and the insulted Tapestry while being groomed by Daff. She looked at Arne. She hadn't been out in the canoe since Adelaide arrived. "What about me?" she demanded.

Arne stared. "Well, what about you?"

She stamped an enraged bare foot. "I like canoeing too, you know," she reminded him waspishly.

"Oh." He regarded her with faint surprise, as if just noticing her existence but without much interest. "All right," he offered grudgingly, "you can borrow the canoe some time when I'm not using it, if you're careful."

Felicity went bang. "Oh!" she exploded. "You—you cultus komox! I just hate you, Arne Knudsen!" Tapestry spat agreement. They both flounced back up the hill in a fury. Barf, who knew very well he wasn't wanted canoeing, bounded eagerly after them, to the great relief of Adelaide. Daffodil sat and regarded her disconcertingly. Arne stared after them, scratching his straw-coloured cowlick in genuine perplexity.

"Now what's wrong with her?" he demanded. Flit had been strange lately. Meek and grumpy by turns, with flashes of perfectly unreasonable temper. It was too bad, when she had seemed to be improving a bit.

He turned with relief to Adelaide, who was smiling tolerantly. "Poor F'licity!" said Adelaide, watching the stormy small figure stamping up the slope.

Felicity reached the house, stomped inside, stood glaring for a moment at nothing in particular, and then snatched the tin bucket from its place by the cupboard and her rifle from the wall. "I'm going berry-picking," she said snappishly to Aunt Julia, and stalked out again. Still followed by Tapestry and Barf, she stalked across the clearing and into the dim green light of the forest, fuming. The animals, picking up her mood, growled softly at each other.

Ooh, how she hated that Arne Knudsen! For months he had scorned and teased her for being useless; and then, when she made herself useful and independent, he turned right around and worshipped the perfect Adelaide, who—who—

Felicity stopped directly in front of a loaded blackberry bush and didn't even see it. Why—Adelaide was every bit as helpless and useless as Felicity had been! Moreover, she was a scare-cat, which Felicity never was. Which meant—surely—that Adelaide wasn't altogether superior, after all, only beautiful! And somehow she hoaxed everyone into—into believing—It was an astonishing discovery! Felicity stood perfectly still contemplating it.

The serenity of the woodland, with its shadowed green depths pierced and flecked with spears of golden sunlight, began to soothe her flayed feelings. Her mood softened from towering fury to astonished indignation. Barf, relieved, slurped his wet-flannel tongue helpfully over Tapestry, who indignantly began cleaning the soaked bit, and then philosophically transferred her tongue to his chest. Presently they were grooming each other with earnest attention. Felicity didn't even notice. Wading recklessly through a patch of nettles, she began to pick the tiny tangy wild blackberries. Her bare ankles stung to match her mood, but not much. Nettles hardly bothered Felicity. They blistered Arne. She smiled with dark satisfaction., and considered nettles in his bed. But another thought crowded into her mind, hardly believable to someone who'd spent her life in the shade of a perfect cousin.

If Adelaide wasn't superior, Felicity need never again try to live up to her!

A silky little skunk who was probably Miss Muffet wandered fearlessly along a mossy log in front of her, white-striped tail high. Barf—who really knew better because of unfortunate experience—nevertheless made a small threat in his throat. Miss Muffet, secure in her supreme defence, didn't even bother to look around. Tapestry, on the other hand, delicately came up to the skunk with a small 'prrt?' of greeting, and they touched noses. Felicity paid little attention. Her mind was on a life-shaking new idea.

She need no longer try to be like Adelaide—or even feel that she ought to try! Never ever again! Why should she? She didn't even want to be! This second heretical discovery caused her to sit down on the log next to Miss Muffet and take a deep breath. Well, she'd like to look like Adelaide, of course; who wouldn't? But that was impossible. As for being like her—She didn't want to sit around and have things done for her. And, now that she was deep into sacrilege, she didn't see why her cousin should get away with being a parasite just because she was beautiful. Not that Felicity could ever convince the others, of course, or have the temerity to try. But why not fight back on her own? Why not whittle Miss Superior down to size? Not to mention the revolting Arne.

An inquisitive rabbit nose poked out from a bush. Barf barked, Tapestry crouched, but it was probably Felicity's smile of diabolical glee that caused it to vanish in alarm. Arne—who was lovesick, and who had also taught Felicity most of the finer points of teasing! She knew his vulnerable points, too! As for Adelaide, who was afraid of everything ...

Why on earth had she been just moping around? There was much to do! Jumping cheerfully to her feet, she began picking berries. Having declared independence and war in the same moment, she would now celebrate by baking blackberry pies.

No one knew what had got into Felicity. She who had always been so humbly admiring of her lovely cousin, now went out of her way to be downright rude and patronizing. And she needled Arne endlessly and without mercy, not seeming to care how many jibes she received in return. Charles, at first, rather enjoyed the feud, but Aunt Julia—not to mention Adelaide—was deeply distressed, and her husband was of no help whatever.

"Not getting along?" Arne heard him say to Aunt Julia. "F'licity and Arne? Oh, just growing pains. They always did squabble, but they really like each other fine. I shouldn't worry, dear."

Arne, smarting from Flit's latest barbed remark, profoundly disagreed. He didn't like her in the least. He'd had nothing but growing pains from that pesky brat from the first, and enough was enough. Personally, he favored some strong discipline applied in the place which nature had thoughtfully provided for it, only no one ever would, of course.

The war continued right into the autumn. And it didn't make things any easier for Arne when he realized that his best friend disloyally took Flit's side!

They were seated on a newly cut log one warm afternoon, resting from the effort of tree-chopping. Across the clearing, a slim barefooted figure appeared for an instant at the cabin door, tossed out a bowl of water, and stood for a moment staring across the lake. "Klahowya, Flit," called Qualchan warmly, ignoring the fact that Arne was ignoring Felicity.

She turned and smiled—selectively at Qualchan. "Klahowya, Qulchan. Stay there a minute," she added and vanished into the house.

"You marry some day?" Qualchan suggested hopefully, glinting out of the corner of his eye at his friend.

"Qualchan!" roared Arne, outraged.

Qualchan, who knew his feelings on that score very well, grinned sheepishly, hesitated, then spoke his mind. "She is good tenas klootchman," he said doggedly. "The other is pretty like trillium, but trillium no use except to look at. Flit good inside, like you. Also," he pointed out practically, "she good cook."

Arne uprooted an unoffending wild godetia. "You just don't know Adelaide very well," he growled.

Qualchan looked at him. Arne, reminded uncomfortably of how Adelaide behaved with Indians, turned red and pulled up a salmon berry. She did act is if they were all grizzlies—even Qualchan, whom she'd seen often, ever since July—Or used to. He didn't come every day any longer, but still—You'd think by now—Arne, realizing his thoughts were veering toward disloyalty if not sacrilege, scowled furiously. "She's just not used to things yet," he muttered.

Qualchan didn't point out that Flit had never behaved that way, not even that first day when Bit shoved dried clams in her face. He didn't need to. He just looked across the slope at the gingham figure which had reappeared holding a huge slab of blackberry pie in each hand and a wide streak of juice down one cheek. Arne got the point, and it didn't at all improve his temper.

Felicity arrived, grinned at Qualchan, and handed him the biggest piece. "Muck-a-muck hiyu klosh, tillicum,'" she grinned, and turned to Arne. "I suppose you can have some, too—this time. Though you really should let Adelaide do your cooking for you."

It was another last straw, and it wiped any vestige of a thank-you out of his head. "I hope your pie's cleaner than your face," he remarked cuttingly as he reached for it.

Felicity gave him the look of one whose feeding hand has just been ungratefully bitten. She pulled the pie out of his reach. She looked at it thoughtfully. She slapped his face with it.

"My face is cleaner than yours, anyhow," she pointed out with bitter satisfaction, and stalked away, sun-streaked head high and full skirt swinging jerkily above slender ankles. Qualchan regarded his klosh tillicum's glaring berry-covered face. He choked with laughter. Then he crowded it back, composed himself, shook his black head, and took a bite of pie. It was delicious.

Felicity went back to the house, gathered her cats, and brooded. "You wouldn't let anyone treat you like that, would you?"

Daffodil, who probably would, so long as it didn't disturb his sleep, yawned. But the feisty Tapestry, sensing her agitation, produced the love-chirp reserved for Felicity, and then growled softly in her throat. Felicity took this as encouragement, and went on the warpath harder than ever.

The trouble was, everyone was against her but the cats and Barf; and only Tapestry, she felt, was really on her side. Aunt Julia scolded her for picking quarrels and making things unpleasant for everyone, while Adelaide would listen with a martyred but forgiving smile that inspired Felicity to thoughts of murder. Even the uncommitted Charles got tired of the show, and pointed out that Adelaide never said insulting things to Felicity, so why—?

Felicity smouldered. Of course Adelaide didn't! She would never put herself in the wrong; she was much too sneaky for that! What no one else ever saw were the pitying glances, the slightly lifted eyebrows, the faint contemptuous shrugs that instantly made Felicity feel stupid, plain, awkward, unladylike, and indistinguishable from White Trash. And in addition, Adelaide always had Arne to battle for her. And he (though Felicity dearly hoped he didn't suspect it) could hurt her more than anyone, especially when he wasn't even trying. And all she knew to do was pretend not to care, and try to get even.

"How nice of you to come to dinner, Cousin," she said sweetly as Arne gallantly pulled Adelaide's stool to the supper table. "Would you like him to feed you, too?"

Adelaide gave her one of those withering Looks. Wondering pity, mixed with faint distaste. As always, it reduced Felicity to something abject and uncouth. No one else saw it, of course: they thought she was being sweetly forbearing. Adelaide had been of late cultivating that look especially for Felicity, and her glinted glance was blandly triumphant. It was, thought Felicity darkly, a sneaky way to fight. She lost her head.

"Why don't you go out and make friends with the other weasels?" she blazed, and deliberately dropped a bot baked potato in her cousin's lap.

Adelaide screamed. Arne (not entirely by accident) knocked Felicity flat in leaping to his lady's rescue. Barf rushed inside barking furiously and knocking Charles' plate to the floor. Charles used some words that had not been in his vocabulary before he went to work at Yesler's. Aunt Julia scolded. Tapestry shot under the table, screeeched that she and Felicity were Being Persecuted, and bit the nearest ankle. It turned out to be Arne's. He yelped. Daff, rudely awakened, yowled protest. Jonathan, speechless, seriously wondered if this was really the happy family he had assumed it was. Felicity flatly refused to apologize and was sent to bed, where she lay listening to them eat the meal she had cooked, and wrathfully thought up ways to get even.

Morning continued on the same disagreeable note. Felicity, up early to soothe her wounded feelings with a nice lonely paddle on the lake before breakfast, had just started to get in the canoe when there was an angry shout from up the hill.

"Get out of my canoe!" yelled Arne. "Who gave you leave?"

Felicity flushed under her tan, and then saw Adelaide, dimpling and yawning, just behind him. Blue eyes smiled into humiliated brown ones, who had been caught wrong-footed and knew it. Defiantly, Felicity knelt in the canoe, and shoved out into the lapping water. Arne tore down the hill and into the lake like a raging grizzly, Felicity faced him like an equally raging cougar, and there was a brief but stimulating battle which involved a great deal of splashing. It ended with both of them getting ducked and starting to laugh—

And then Adelaide wailed that F'licity had deliberately got her all soaking wet. Arne fired up again, led his abused lady up to the house, and told Felicity with deep earnestness what he'd do if she ever again touched his canoe.

Unfortunately, Felicity couldn't start a full war yet, for there was breakfast to get, and she couldn't leave Aunt Julia do it alone, so she followed. And then they discovered that the fire had gone out during the night. Everyone blamed everyone (especially Arne and Felicity) for not having banked it properly, and it required flint, steel and considerable time before there could be any cooking.

And then Adelaide produced the final straw for Felicity. She was all honey and gracious forgiveness by breakfast, causing Charles to remark acidly that it was nice to have some folk in the house who didn't go around holding grudges. Felicity shot him a poisonous look, but Adelaide put on her air of Christian Charity.

"Now Charles, honey, you mustn't pick on poor F'licity; some folks just aren't sweet-tempered by nature. And you know she does some things I just couldn't. Imagine her going out in that wild forest by herself, and shooting a rifle and all, just like an Indian."

The rest of the family, taking this as compliment and peace-pipe, beamed at Adelaide and looked expectantly at Felicity. Felicity, knowing concealed insults when she heard them, looked like Tapestry contemplating attack. Uncle Jon, failing to notice this, turned to her.

"Why don't you take Adelaide out for a walk in the woods some day, F'licity? I believe she'd come to love it as much as you do, once she got to know it. And I expect you'd both like to get off by yourselves for some girl-talk.

Felicity, revolted by the idea, opened her mouth to say so. Then common sense worked its way into her head. Why should she go on behaving just as Addie wanted her to, and getting all the blame? In fact—

A lovely fiendish idea came to her.

"All right," she agreed with a bright smile that only Adelaide recognized as being as false as her own. "We'll go today if you'd like, Adelaide."

Adelaide wished to decline rudely, but as an experienced strategist, she knew when she was in danger of being out-maneuvered. F'licity was not going to steal the role of gracious and noble and sweet-tempered peacemaker. Her smile became even more angelic than her cousin's. "How sweet of you, F'licity! I'd love to go with you, honey, but I'd jus' be too scared."

"Nonsense, of course you must go," said Aunt Julia, who was rather less naive about her daughter than was Jonathan. "If Felicity had to learn from scratch, and she sickly as she was, you can surely learn with her to help you."

"Oh, yes!" Felicity agreed artlessly. "I do want you to come, most awfully," she added with truth, and watched her cousin's face from the corner of her eye.

Adelaide discovered that she had been out-maneuvered after all. She couldn't back down now without losing the upper hand. F'licity was developing a right sneaky mind! Vowing never to let this happen again, Adelaide conceded this one trick.

"Why, honey," she crooned. "You know I'd do jus' anything to make you happy! Of course we'll take a walk in the woods if you want it so badly."

"Good!" said her cousin with unnerving alacrity. "We'll go this afternoon while the weather holds." And her pleasure at the prospect was perfectly and obviously genuine.

CHAPTER 13

▼

CROW'S WARNING

The two girls stepped into the flickering emerald of the forest, which closed about them in a green sea of ferns and bracken and trees. None of the animals chose to join them, Daffodil being asleep, Tapestry out hunting gophers, and Barf with Arne. The wildlife rejoiced at this. A splash of bird-song tossed overhead, and a long-tailed pheasant ran heavily under the nearest huckleberry bush. Adelaide cast a nervous glance behind her, clearly on the verge of backing out. But Felicity didn't intend to be balked of her pleasant plans.

"It's perfectly safe," she said bracingly. "You don't want Arne to think you a scare-cat, do you? Come on, I want to show you a lovely place where we can pick wildflowers, and then sit down and rest if you've a mind."

Her soothing tones caused Adelaide to rally at once. "Oh, well, if it's not too far," she patronized. "You mustn't forget, honey, that this is still a wilderness."

Felicity smiled through her teeth and became almost motherly. "I've got my rifle, you know, so you mustn't fret. Right this way, Adelaide."

'This way' just happened to be through a patch of nettles which Felicity had spotted several yards away. She bore her own stings stoically, knowing that the the tiny blisters on her bare ankles would be gone in an hour or two. Adelaide had only a few stings through her stockings, but with any luck, they might last for days.

A little farther on, Miss Muffet sauntered out from the underbrush, gave Adelaide a very disparaging glance, and leaned against Felicity's ankle. Adelaide gawked.

"F'licity, that's—Isn't that a skunk?

Felicity had never been fonder of Muffet. She stooped and stroked her head. "Yes. of course. You want to stay back, honey, but skunks do like me, and this is a particular friend of mine," she said with a gloriously unbearable air of superiority which almost made up for past humiliation. "Come on, then; don't just stand there looking silly."

That almost finished Adelaide—but Felicity wanted to make sure. So she led them through devil's club (being careful only to touch the tops of the leaves, herself), and Adelaide, one hand looking like a pincushion, promptly lost all pretense at enthusiasm or even sportsmanship. "I want to go back right now, F'licity Ann Dare; y'hear me?"

But Felicity had tasted the sweetness of vengeance, and not even a certain thrashing would have persuaded her to forego an instant of the rest of the venture. "I don't feel like it," she pointed out callously. "You can try it, Addie, but I reckon you'd get lost for sure."

So did Adelaide, who lagged sullenly behind the cruel pace on up the steep hill, through thick slashing underbrush. Soon she was panting. She had pitch on her hands and clothes, and a rip in her skirt. Her golden curls had been pulled out of their net and tangled by hostile branches, and she had discovered several more patches of nettles without any cousinly assistance.

Felicity beamed. This was the most fun she'd had since the cats had come in from the rain. Once they reached the top of the hill, she could announce that they were lost, and let Adelaide have conniption fits for a while, and serve her right for being so stupid. Even if she hadn't Felicity's remarkable sense of direction, she should know by now that all it needed was to go down hill until she found either a creek or the lake.

Near the top, they came to a small glade where long jewel-green grass had made a small foothold for itself in the midst of greedy underbrush. Around it, Oregon grape flaunted holly-like leaves and dark blue berries, and on one side stood a massive maple tree with several trunks. And on all sides giant firs stabbed their tips into the sky. Felicity forgot the trailing Adelaide for a moment. How lovely! Robins flirted fearlessly over a moss-covered log at the center of the glade. A bluejay swore at her from a high black-trunked dogwood that had finished its giant ivory flowers; and from a distance crows scolded harshly and incessantly.

An elusive memory nagged furtively at Felicity's mind: something to do with crows scolding. But before she could capture it, Adelaide puffed up, much the worse for wear. "This is simply awful, F'licity!" she gasped in breathless outrage. "Every single thing in this dreadful place slaps me or grabs me or sticks me or stings me! I can't go another step!" Contradicting herself briefly, she limped over to the mossy log and sat down on it.

Felicity regarded her with a faint touch of remorse which was instantly killed by Adelaide's next words. "As soon as I've rested, you can take me right home, F'licity Dare! Jus' wait until Father and Arne see what you've done!"

"Oh, sum-muckle!" snapped Felicity. The crows' screaming was getting closer and a bit unnerving. "By the way," she added maliciously, but partly to hide that vague uneasiness even from herself, "I think it was somewhere near here that David Denny saw a big grizzly."

With a stifled cry Adelaide leaped to her feet, tripped over the stub of a branch hidden in the grass, stepped heavily into a hole. Another cry, this one of pain. Felicity instantly forgot hostilities and leaped to her cousin's side.

"I—I've hurt my ankle," said Adelaide in a frightened and oddly apologetic voice. "I—I'm sorry, F'licity."

Laying down her rifle, Felicity helped pull the wrenched foot gently out of the hole, and looked at it anxiously. "Can you move it?"

"A little—but oh! It hurts!"

It was clear that she couldn't walk on it. Not yet, anyway. Felicity firmly pushed panic to the back of her mind, and helped her cousin to sit on the log again. Then she sat still for a moment, thinking furiously. What if the ankle was too badly hurt for Adelaide to get home? She'd just have to shoot off the rifle and hope someone heard, frightening everyone and embarrassing herself.

It was all her fault. She began to dislike herself heartily. She'd reckoned she had a right to get even—but now here was Adelaide being an awfully good sport about it. No reproaches, no tears; just gritted teeth and even a gallant effort to make conversation, though her head was now resting on her knees in pain. "What do you reckon those birds are fussing about?"

In truth, they were almost overhead now, screaming of—The half-memory snapped into focus. Of danger! The crows had been warning; now some other sense did. She sat rigid for an instant, suddenly afraid to look.

It wasn't exactly a movement that caught her eye. She never knew quite what it was. But her gaze was drawn slowly to the right, past Adelaide's lowered head, where a faint animal trail ran past the maple, and a tawny figure slowly formed itself from the shadows of the underbrush—and her mind went blank and disbe-lieving.

A cougar stood there, round-tipped ears flattened slightly over yellow eyes and white muzzle; far larger and more like Shadow than Felicity had even dreamed, and totally terrifying. They stared at each other, girl and mountain lion for a brief eternity, while her heart (more realistic than her dazed mind) thudded fit to break her ribs and choke her.

Random thoughts tumbled through her head. Nobody had told her how extremely large—and how beautiful!—they were. A little section of her mind took a tiny instant to observe the expressive ears, black-tipped tail, white snout, and oddly solemn expression. Another, more practical, part sizzled random thoughts: Her rifle was out of reach on the other side of Adelaide. What would happen if she tried to get to it? ... Or when Adelaide looked up and began to scream? What had Chief Sealth said about cougars? ... All she could remember was not to run away. It still stood watching her, looking for all the world like Shadow the first time he peered reprovingly out of the bush at her; and Felicity was not at all sure she could bring herself to shoot at it, even if she could reach her rifle—or even that it would be a good idea to try. Likely she'd just wound it and make things worse.

The cougar shifted its eyes, lifted one front paw and then the other the way Tapestry sometimes did.—Uncertainly? She was staring at it. She remembered now: cats considered staring to be a threat—but a run-away threat or an attack threat? It rumbled in warning—or complaint—or menace—

Adelaide lifted her head, saw it and began to scream, piercingly and repeat-edly. The cougar's ears swivelled and flattened, and it crouched, staring at the noise-maker.

Felicity found herself praying; not to the unfair God, but to something more appropriate, perhaps Chief Sealth's Earth Spirits. From somewhere came a sense of what to do. Would Adelaide's screams deter or anger it? Surely now it needed calming?

"Quiet, Adelaide!" she snapped in a low voice that somehow penetrated her cousin's terror and silenced her—and moved the cougar's eyes back to her. It was exactly the way Shadow used to look! Felicity found herself talking to it in the same tones.

"Poor thing, are you scared? We wouldn't hurt you, and you don't really want to hurt us, do you? It's all a mistake." She stood unmoving, let her gaze drop to the face rather than the golden eyes. The cougar, confused by such contradictory signals, snarled again, but tentatively. The snarl slowly changed, became

Shadow's pensive expression. Encouraged, Felicity went on talking with more confidence now, though her heart still pounded painfully. Presently, unbelievably, the mountain lion sat down and yawned. Just the way Marilla had done! Felicity was not quite sure whether yawning was a sign of harmlessness or indesiciveness or perhaps both. But she anwered it with a long wide yawn of her own, just as she had done with the feral cats, and let her eyelids droop slowly. The couger tilted its head, the ears lifting and aiming toward her. It yawned again, watched intently as Felicity responded—and then rose, stood watching for a moment, turned, and melted into the underbrush.

Adelaide whimpered and fell back into a huddle. Felicity did very much the same—but with a watchful eye on the maple tree. Presently Adelaide crawled over to her, laughing and crying at once. "Oh, F'licity, F'licity! How could you be so brave? What did you do? You're so wonderful!"

Felicity stared at her and again at the empty space by the maple tree. "Oh, I'm not!" she wailed, and burst into tears. For a moment they clung to each other, sobbing. Then Felicity pulled herself together and reflected that it might be as well to leave just in case Somebody changed its mind.

"Reckon we'd best get back," she said with what she hoped was a matter-of-fact air. "You reckon you could walk a little if you lean hard on me?"

"I'll try," sniffed Adelaide, wiping her cheeks.

It was a brutal nightmarish trip. Down and down, ignoring minor discomforts of thorns and nettles, Felicity discovering the cruelty that the tripping and hampering forest had already demonstrated to her cousin. Time after time they fell together in a wretched heap, to sit gasping until they could rise again. The rifle was abandoned. Adelaide was getting heavier and heavier, and the crows started screaming again, and Felicity listened despairingly to a sound behind the crows, almost audible.

"Adelaide, could you scream again? I'm not very good at it, and I think I hear—" Adelaide, drawing quite the wrong conclusions, obliged, piercingly. And at once she was answered by a frenzy of barking from down the hill and a frantic shout.

"Flit! Flit, where are you?"

"Arne! Here! Help!"

And presently he was there, taking the back-breaking weight of Adelaide, scolding and worrying while Barf cavorted around them, ears and tail flying, totally in the way, but convinced that he had saved the day single-pawed.

"It was a mountain lion," Adelaide told Arne faintly, beginning to cry now in earnest. "It was so dreadful! F'licity just talked to him and made him go away, and saved us. Oh, Arne, she was so brave!"

She said it again when, swollen ankle swathed in cold cloths, she lay on her bed and looked up at her cousin. "You were so wonderful, F'licity! I'll never to my dying day forget the way you told me to be quiet so it wouldn't eat me, and then you jus' stood there and faced that awful monster alone! And after I've— Well—I reckon I've been a mite mean at times …"

Felicity hardly noticed this difficult confession because she was struggling with one of her own. She reached down to where a pair of erect tails wound around her skirts waiting to be stroked. She obliged and looked up.

"I'm not a bit wonderful," she said flatly. "I took you through the nettles and devil's club and all on purpose to make you hate the woods, and I was going to say we were lost, to get you even more scared. I was getting even because you're always looking down on me."

Adelaide sniffed. "Not any more," she quavered. "Didn't you know? I did, back in Virginia, and I used to feel sorry for you; but ever since I got here it's been the other way, and you look down on me and I feel insignificant and no-count because you're good at everything and I can't do anything. And I was just trying to get my own back, and that's the honest truth, F'licity Dare. I still say you're wonderful, and it was magic what you did, and I reckon I could never talk to a mountain lion that way, but—Flit? I'd like for you to teach me to cook and all, and us be friends?"

Felicity stared. It must have been terribly hard for Adelaide to say those things! Felicity didn't think she could have done it. It was a different kind of courage, maybe, from talking to wild cougars. She struggled with herself.

"I reckon you're—I mean—Well—could you teach me to sew?" she asked at last. "I'm still perfectly awful at that."

And with those difficult things said—or at least, for Felicity, half said—it was as if a great hole had been knocked in the wall of jealousy between them. Not that the wall was gone yet—but it had definitely started to crumble.

They looked at each other. They smiled. They burst into tears.

The duet of sobs penetrated the fire-lit main room of the cabin where Charles was still looking stunned while Jon persuaded Julia that it was all over now and they'd take care it never happened again. But at the sound of sobbing, it was he who looked alarmed and started to rise, and his wife who patted his arm placidly.

"Leave them alone," she said. "This is what they need. Lie down and be quiet, Barf. Arne, is that dog going to try to rescue us all every five minutes from now on, you reckon?"

Arne paid no attention. He sat on a stool and glared into the flames, trying to get his feelings figured out. He thought back to the moment he had first heard the screams faintly from that beautiful and dangerous forest. Had his first instinctive thought been of a golden head and blue eyes? Even though he knew perfectly well who was screaming? No. It had not. It had been of wayward short hair with a silly duck-tail at the nape of a slender neck, of brown eyes in an impudent face. "Flit!" he had yelled, and hurled himself toward the sound.

This was all wrong! It was Adelaide who held his heart, not that bad-tempered little pest who needed spanking—wasn't it? Arne blinked. He examined his heart. Holy Moses!

The sound of sobs was subsiding as he raised a confused head, absently patted Barf's erect ear, and stared blankly toward the bedroom. Frowning a little, he went to the doorway and looked in. On her bed a creamy petal face mopped its eyes and looked up, all the lovelier for the recent storm. Yes, Adelaide was definitely a fairy-tale princess, sweet and winsome, born to be adored and protected … Beside the bed a cropped tangled head raised itself over a tapestried feline who growled at Arne. The back of a grubby hand dug into reddened eyes. Tears did not become Flit. She regarded him with a mixture of defiance and apology. Any moment, the apology would turn to sassiness and she would be back to her independent infuriating self. It was a very different self from the baby-doll of even a year ago.

"Well?" Felicity stuck out a truculent lower lip.

Arne looked at her. He cleared his throat. He paid her the very highest compliment he could think of.

"For a girl," he said gruffly, "you're almost as good as a boy."

Felicity stiffened, bridled, and then smirked. "I'm better," she retorted, smug. I can tame wild animals. *And* I can cook, too."

The End

Historical Note

This is a true story about the start of Seattle. I grew up there, and all the descriptions of the countryside, the weather, the forest and bay, and settlers are quite accurate. Chinook was a real trade jargon—and the warm wind called the chinook does go to the head. And as Arne predicted, even today the streets north of Yesler Way head northwest with the shoreline, while those to the south follow the compass.

Only the Dare family, Arne, Qualchan, Bit and Satco—and the animals—are imaginary.

Oregon Territory was indeed separated into Washington and Oregon, and Governor Stevens arranged an Indian conference in front of Doc Maynard's store: the tribes of Duwamish, Snohomish, Puyallup, Skagit, and all. He told them what the Great White Father had decided was good for them, and gave them no choice but to accept. It was then that Chief Sealth made his famous speech, accepting, foretelling the disappearance of his people. Dr. Smith, who was so sympathetic to the Indians that he had learned Duwamish, translated it, so his is probably the most accurate of the four different versions. Here are parts of it.

Yonder sky, which has wept tears of compassion on our fathers for centuries untold, and which, to us, looks eternal, may change. Today it is fair, tomorrow it may be overcast with clouds. My words are like the stars that never set ...

The son of the white chief says his father sends us greetings of friendship and good will. This is kind, for we know he has little need of our friendship in return, because his people are many. They are like the grass that covers the vast prairies, while my people are few, and resemble the scattering trees of a storm-swept plain ...

It matters little where we pass the remainder of our days. They are not many. The Indian's night promises to be dark. No bright star hovers about the horizon. Sad-voiced winds moan in the distance. Some grim Nemesis of our race is on the red man's trail, and wherever he goes he will still hear the sure approaching footsteps of the fell destroyer. A few more moons, a few more winters, and not one of all the mighty hosts that once filled this broad land will remain to weep over the tombs of a people once as powerful and as hopeful as your own.

But why should we repine? Why should I murmur at the fate of my people? Tribes are made up of individuals and are no better than they. Men come and go like the waves of the sea. A tear, a tamanamus, a dirge, and they are gone from our longing eyes forever. Even the white man, whose God walked and talked with his people, is not exempt from the common destiny. We may be brothers, after all. We shall see.

We will ponder your proposition, and when we have decided, we will tell you. But should we accept it, I here and now make this the first condition: that we will not be denied the privilege, without molestation, of visiting at will the graves of our ancestors and friends. Every part of this country is sacred to my people. Every hillside, every valley, every plain and grove has been hallowed by some fond memory or some sad experience of my tribe.

And when the last red man shall have perished from the earth and his memory among white men shall have become a myth, these shores shall still swarm with the invisible dead of my tribe; and when your children's children shall think themselves alone in the field, the store, upon the highway or in the silence of the woods, they will not be alone. In all the earth there is no place dedicated to solitude. At night, when the streets of your towns shall be silent and you think deserted, they will throng with the returning hosts that once filled and still love this beautiful land. The white man will never be alone. Let him be just and deal kindly with muy people, for the dead are not altogether powerless.

And so we go our separate ways: you to new power and conquest, we to death.

Did I say death? There is no death; only a change of worlds.

But as Mrs. Bell predicted, the white man was incapable of dealing fairly with the Indian, and broke the treaty almost before it was signed. In his report to the Office of Indian Affairs later that year, Governor Stevens wrote this: The speedy extinction of the race seems rather to be hoped for than regretted, and they look forward to it themselves with a sort of indifference.

Inevitably even the peaceful Duwamish were driven into war—and inevitably they were beaten and driven back to the inadequate waterless (in Washington!)

reservations alloted to them. And most of the settlers, now afraid of their once-friends, turned against them. Doc Maynard was now called Indian-lover.

As Sealth aged, he spent most of his time with his people in the reservation across Puget Sound, but he kept his friendship with Doc. He died of a heart attack in 1866.

I was never taught the history of Seattle at school. Possibly a belated sense of guilt made it embarrassing? At any rate, we knew only rough dates and no details. And as for the Indians—when I was young we used to see "The Siwashes" (which I believed until researching this boook was the name of a tribe) crossing on the ferry to pick strawberries, drab, huddled, defeated, without pride or hope.

When I first wrote Poor Felicity in 1960, I was young and ignorant, and I had Felicity show her courage by shooting the poor cougar. I've always regretted that—especially after learning more about cougars. They aren't basically aggressive: mostly just very curious and often friendly—like any cat. Here in the city of Santa Rosa they show up regularly, sometimes half a mile or less from my home, and have never attacked anyone, even though they wander into our gardens or on porches—partly because we're pushing them out of their territory and they're hunting food. (This, admittedly, can be hard on unwary pets—but if you're hungry, you're hungry. Humans, too, will do what ever it takes to eat.) But cougars are often seen just peering curiously into windows to see what's going on.

I've also personally experienced the baby skunks coming to play, and Miss Muffet (whom I actually named Little Dorrit); and having spent years in a cat rescue group, I understand about taming ferals.

So what with one thing and another, this version of Poor Felicity is much more animal-friendly than the first.

Chinook Glossary

Boston	English, American, European
chako	come
chuck	water
cultus	no-good
hiyu	much, very
hyak	quick
hyas	big
Hyas Chuck	Lake Washington
itka	what
klahowya	hello or goodby
klootchman	woman
klosh	good
komox	dog
mahsie	thank you
makook	sell
Makook House	Dr. Maynard's general store
mamook	make
mamook memaloose	make dead, kill
memaloose	dead
massachie	wicked

mika	you
muck-a-muck	food
nesika	see
nika	I, me
pooh	bang
salt chuck	sea
Siwash	Indian (a corruption of 'savage'!)
skookum	strong, brave
skookum chuck	river
solecks	angry
sum-muckle	shut up
tenas	little
Tenas Chuck	Lake Union
tenaas klootchman	little girl
tenas sun	morning
tickey	want
tillicum	friend

1220919

Made in the USA